Vargas saw smoke curling up from the Uzi's unseeing eye

The gunner loomed above him like a giant, bending over and speaking softly, barely loud enough for Vargas to make out the words.

"I'm back. Somebody knows why. Spread the word."

Then something fell onto Vargas's chest, making him flinch and close his eyes, ready for death. But when he opened them a moment later, he was all alone—with the dead.

Fighting off the pain, he craned his neck to look down, squinting at the object glittering on his bloody shirtfront. In an instant he knew precisely what it was, but dared not hope to grasp its meaning.

The shiny metal disc was a marksman's medal.

MACK BOLAN

The Executioner

DON·PENDLETON's EXECUTIONER

MACK BOLAN

Blood Dues

A GOLD EAGLE BOOK FROM

WORLDWIDE

TORONTO · NEW YORK · LONDON · PARIS
AMSTERDAM · STOCKHOLM · HAMBURG
ATHENS · MILAN · TOKYO · SYDNEY

First edition November 1984

ISBN 0-373-61071-8

Special thanks and acknowledgment to
Mike Newton for his contributions to this work.

Printed in Canada

If you want to serve God, you have to take on His attributes. That includes the heavy responsibility of exercising vengeance.
—*Norman Mailer*

Some call the Mafia a second government. Right. Well, if that's the case, there's going to be a second Civil War—
The Executioner vs the Mob.
—*Mack Bolan*

PROLOGUE

The warrior was at home in darkness, comfortable in a world of gliding shadows. Motionless, he listened to the night noises all around him, picking out the sounds of insects, night birds, an alligator rumbling for its mate across the marshy hummocks. The soldier melded with the environment of the steaming Everglades, a predator like those around him, seeking prey in the gloom.

But he would not find it there.

The jungle compound was long abandoned. Weeds and clinging vines had overgrown the clapboard barracks structures, creepers tangling in the uprights of the one remaining lookout tower. Barbed-wire fencing, collapsed and rotted through in spots to grant him easy access, had become a rusty trellis for the climbing undergrowth.

The compound was deserted, yes, but it was still alive. The weathered buildings were infested now by furtive, creeping things, and swamp birds roosted in the sole surviving tower. Man had given way to the relentless march of Mother Nature there, but he had also left his brand upon the Everglades.

And there were ghosts.

The warrior felt them as he passed inside the fence, encroaching on their territory. If he closed his eyes, it almost seemed that he might see them, moving in and out around the barracks, standing their eternal watch along the overgrown perimeter.

He heard their voices whispering to him on the night wind, here disguised as rustling leaves, there the gentle creaking of intertwined trunks of swamp trees. They spoke to him in urgent terms; of honor, duty, vengeance, calling him by name.

The warrior answered them, and stilled their soft demanding voices with a promise.

Soon, soldados.

He was home again, among the ghosts, and there were dues to pay.

In blood.

1

The meet was on. John Hannon had been working toward it now for six long weeks, and he could not deny the tingle of excitement at knowing it was really set. With any luck, he would have enough to put the whole thing under wraps tonight. Enough, perhaps, to get the D.A. off his ass and into action.

Waiting for the elevator, Hannon impatiently checked his digital Timex again. Five minutes later than the last time and two hours left to kill. The drive would use up half of that, and he could find a restaurant along the way to kill the other hour.

It occurred to Hannon that he had not eaten well in several days, but he would make up for it soon. The old excitement of the hunt was bringing back his appetite.

It was like old times—well, almost—fitting all the scrambled pieces into place and making sense of jumbled, fragmentary leads. So different from the routine background checks and tawdry marital investigations that had largely occupied his days since he retired from Homicide.

This time, it seemed to count for something.

He had never met the Cuban, never even heard his voice before the call came in that afternoon, but he had instantly agreed to a meeting. The risk was there, of course—there was enough of the policeman left in Hannon to prepare him for the worst—but he was too damned close to pass.

At last the elevator came, and Hannon rode the five floors down alone. Inside the office building's basement parking lot, the atmosphere was stale; it smelled of gasoline and motor oil. Alighting from the elevator, Hannon glanced both ways, saw nothing out of place, and moved out briskly toward his Buick three aisles over.

He had reached the car, his key in the lock, before he felt the enemy behind him. There was something, like the prickling of gooseflesh on his back, that signaled danger close at hand. He suddenly felt cornered in the parking stall. He was half prepared to turn when polished steel was pressed against the back of his skull.

John Hannon recognized the feel of gunmetal and he froze. The subterranean garage no longer smelled like stale exhaust; instead, he thought it smelled of death.

"You know the drill," a husky voice informed him.

Hannon knew the drill, all right. He had been on the other end of it perhaps a thousand times. Both hands upon the Buick's roof, his feet well back and shoulder width apart. A pair of hands explored him expertly, relieving him of the two-inch .38 he carried on his hip, and still the pistol pressed against his skull.

So there were two of them.

"He's clean," a second voice announced.

A strong hand on his shoulder spun him around, then shoved him back against the Buick. There *were* two of them, like lethal bookends in their carbon-copy suits and modish haircuts. Hannon recognized the older of the two—his name was Joey something—but his effort to recall the rest of it was hampered by their weapons.

Joey Something held a Smith and Wesson .357 leveled at his chest. His partner clutched the snubby Colt that he had lifted out of Hannon's holster. At that range, Hannon realized, it would not matter which they used.

"We're going for a ride," the older gunman told him. "You're driving."

Hannon nodded.

"Get behind the wheel and don't try any hero bull-shit."

Hannon did as he was told, aware that he was momentarily in a no-win situation. If he tried to flee on foot, or to start the engine prematurely, they would have him in a deadly cross fire. He would never stand a chance.

The older gunman's name was still elusive, but some fragments of his rap sheet had been filtering back. Extortion. . .arson. . .murder.

He was Mafia, a "made guy," right.

It figured.

Joey Something crawled in on the passenger's side, while his companion settled in the back seat, covering Hannon from behind.

"Where to?"

"I'll let you know," the front-seat gunner told him. "Get on Seventh, going south. And take it easy."

Hannon got the Buick rolling, followed orders as he pulled out of the garage, merging with the traffic. A sleek black Firebird almost cut him off, but Hannon forged ahead, refusing to be buffaloed. The sportster fell in line behind him, any parting gesture from its driver hidden by the tinted windshield.

Bearing south, they passed the twenty-story Omni, new Miami's unofficial centerpiece. The shotgun rider guided him beneath the 395 interchange and past the gently rolling greenery of Bicentennial Park, the ocean on their left now.

A group of tanned, bikini-clad girls were playing Frisbee on the grass, and Hannon felt a pang that pierced him like a knife. It struck him as obscene that children should be playing games while he was on his way to die.

The gunners meant to kill him, Hannon was certain. This had all the earmarks of a classic one-way ride, its only consolation being final proof that he was getting close. *So close* . . . .

Survival was the first priority, and Hannon's mind was occupied with the mechanics of escape. They'd be heading out of town—away from any crowds—and there was a chance that he could get away when they cleared the heavy downtown traffic. He could bail out, risking any oncoming vehicles. There was a chance, if he could take the *mafiosi* by surprise.

If their reaction time was slow enough to let him leave the speeding car alive.

If no one driving home from work plowed him under like a rabbit on the highway.

The grim alternative was certain death, and Hannon had already come to terms with that reality. If all else failed, he was determined now to take the gunmen with him. He would smash the Buick into anything available—a bridge abutment or a semirig—before he let them lead him like a lamb to slaughter.

Suddenly it came to him.

The gunner's name was Joey Stompanato.

Hannon's memories were flooding back as if the file lay open on a desk in front of him. They called him Joey

Stomps, a nickname dating back to when he used to muscle for the local shylocks, breaking legs and skulls as an enforcer for the mob's elite collection agency. He was suspected of a dozen homicides in Florida alone, but Stompanato's only time inside had been the thirty days he served for battery in the sixties.

Joey Stomps was lethal, right. And at the moment, he belonged to Tommy Drake.

That told the ex-detective everything he had to know, and it increased his grim resolve to take the killers with him as a last resort.

They were merging onto Flagler, running to the west, when Hannon spied the tail. His back-seat passenger had shifted, and Hannon saw the Firebird shadowing them. It might have been coincidence, or Stompanato was professional enough to bring a backup team, in case of some mishap. If there were other guns behind them, then his freedom leap was doomed before he made the effort. Even if the crash got Stompanato and his sidekick, number two would swerve and crush the life from Hannon as he bounced across the street.

Okay. The enemy was closing out his options, leaving him with only one alternative.

The traffic started thinning out, and Hannon took advantage of it, tromping on the accelerator. Stompanato jammed the .357 Magnum hard against the ex-detective's ribs, thumbing back the hammer.

"Slow down, goddammit! We're not taking any tickets."

Hannon grinned and kept the pedal down. *Don't worry, Stomps, you bought your ticket when you came aboard. One-way, to the end of the line.*

Hannon could feel the muzzle of his own Colt still

jammed between his shoulders from behind, and he braced himself to take the bullet.

"Ease off, you bastard!"

Hannon laughed at Stompanato, recognized the crackle of incipient hysteria in his voice.

Stompanato's sidekick had the rearview mirror blocked, his face a twisted panic mask, but Hannon caught the Firebird in the side mirror now, approaching and about to overtake them on the left.

The starboard window powered down, and Hannon glimpsed a flash of steel inside as a pistol leveled into target acquisition. The ex-cop had a flash impression of a single, solemn face, a spill of raven hair across the forehead as the driver sighted down the barrel.

Stompanato's backup was alone, and even as Hannon registered the oddity of that, he pushed the riddle from his mind. A quarter mile ahead of them, a freeway overpass provided him with what he needed, massive concrete pylons waiting to receive the hurtling Buick.

Hannon hunched his shoulders, leaning toward the steering wheel as if his posture might extract another mile or two per hour from the straining engine. He never really felt the blow that Stompanato landed on his ribs.

Out of the corner of his eye he saw the Firebird's sleek nose lining up with the Buick's, and he waited for the bullet to core his skull. The backup man would panic, try to stop him with a flying shot, and the ex-policeman was gratified to know it would not matter in the least. When he died, the Buick would continue on for a hundred yards or so before his dead weight locked the steering wheel and sent them over in a devastating barrel roll.

All that flashed through Hannon's mind within a

heartbeat, vividly emblazoned on the mental viewing screen—and none of it took place.

There was no shot. Instead the Firebird pulled away, outdistancing the Buick and leaving them behind.

Abruptly, up ahead, the sportster cut in front of him, its brake lights winking on. Instinctively, John Hannon hit the brakes and cranked the wheel around to avoid the collision, veering right and off the pavement. They plowed across the shoulder, and a grassy bank was looming up ahead of them before he had a chance to realize that he was losing it.

The Buick started climbing, drive wheels chewing turf and spitting gravel. They were drifting, sliding, slowly losing ground, the engine choking, stalling out.

They had him.

Hannon knew it, and something snapped inside of him. He lashed at Stompanato with a backhand, ripping his knuckles on the gunner's teeth. Then the ex-cop found the door latch, wrenching at it, spilling out onto the grass.

The Smith & Wesson roared behind him, and he felt its fiery breath against his cheek before he tumbled momentarily out of range. The heavy bullet pushed its shock waves past his face.

And he was scrambling on his hands and knees now, struggling to gain his feet and knowing if he did that he would make a perfect target for the pistoleros.

In his panic, Hannon saw the third man only as a shadow, moving up the bank with loping strides. The ex-detective tried to veer away and lost his balance, sprawling, rolling over on his back.

The new arrival reached him, passed him, breaking for the Buick with an autoloading pistol in his fist. Beyond him, Joey Stompanato was a hulking silhouette emerging from the driver's door, his Magnum probing emptying air.

The newcomer hit a crouch and snapped his automatic out to full arm's length, the weapon's silencer emitting muffled popping sounds. The Stomper crumpled backward, streaming liquid traces of himself across the inside of the windshield.

The stranger pivoted, acquiring target number two before the back-seat gunner realized exactly what was happening. A single bullet struck the Buick's window, drilled on through and pulped the hit man's face. He disappeared without a sound.

The sole surviving shooter doubled back, already holstering the autoloader underneath his jacket.

"Time to go," he said. "You ready, Hannon?"

2

"Do we know each other?"

Mack Bolan, in the driver's seat, glanced over at his passenger.

"We've never met," he answered.

They had never met face to face, but in the early days of Bolan's war against the Mafia their paths had crossed. John Hannon was a captain of detectives then, determined to abort the latest efforts of a hellfire warrior who was taking on the Mob alone. The captain had led the riot squad, responding after Bolan had dropped in uninvited on a syndicate convention in Miami. But the police skipper had come too late, arriving just in time to help pick up the pieces from a strike that left the *mafiosi* reeling, locally and nationwide.

The man who sat beside Mack Bolan now was different, aged. It showed around his eyes, in graying hair and in the hard set of his mouth. He was a man with troubles, right, and Hannon's problems were a part of what had brought the Executioner back again to southern Florida.

"You saved my ass back there," John Hannon said. "I owe you one."

"You owe me nothing."

"Well, I'd like to shake your hand, at least." They shook, and Hannon's grip was solid, firm. "At the risk of sounding like an ingrate...why'd you do it? I mean, who the hell *are* you?''

Bolan had the answer ready. "Frank LaMancha. And you seemed worth saving."

"Are you federal?"

"Not exactly," Bolan answered, skating in as close to candor as he dared. "I think we have a common interest."

Hannon chewed on that a moment staring out the window, finally deciding not to push it.

When he broke his silence Hannon said, "I'll have to make a call about the shooting. Metro won't take long to trace my car."

The Executioner was well ahead of him.

"I'll drop you at a pay phone, but we need to talk before you make that call."

"That right?" The ex-detective's tone was skeptical.

"I'm interested in why those two gorillas took you for a ride."

"Well, now, if you're not law enforcement...."

"Did I say that?"

Hannon looked confused.

"I asked...I mean...."

"It's off the record," Bolan told him. "Call it 'need to know.'"

"I see." The former homicide detective's intonation made it clear he did not see at all.

"You know those guys?"

"One of them," Hannon answered, plainly hesitant. "A shooter by the name of Joey Stompanato. He belongs—belonged—to Tommy Drake. That tell you anything."

"It does."

Mack Bolan riffled through his mental mug file, flashing up the entry on one Tommy Drake. He was a middle-ranking *mafioso,* risen through attrition to acquire preeminence in the chaotic drug trade. While not a boss, he had the capability of putting out a contract. But the question still remained of why he bothered with a former captain of detectives.

"What's the tie-in?"

Hannon spent another silent moment staring at the road before he answered.

"Since you know my name, you've got to know I used to be with the Miami Police Department." He waited for the Executioner's confirming nod. "I pulled the pin two years ago, and since then I've been mostly working private."

"Something special in the wind?"

"It didn't start that way." Another thoughtful pause. "I handle some investigations for Miami Mutual—evaluating claims and checking into frauds, that kind of thing. About six weeks ago they put me on a theft of long-haul moving vans."

The former captain of detectives shifted in his seat and cleared his throat before continuing.

"The vans were stolen from a single firm, but when I started checking into it, I learned they weren't the only ones. Turns out we've had a dozen moving vans and semirigs ripped off right here in Dade these past two months."

"Is that unusual?" Bolan asked.

"Damn right. These rigs were empties, mind you, nothing worth a hijack, and they're too conspicuous to keep around for long. I mean, nobody goes for midnight joyrides in a semitractor."

"Someone's moving contraband?"

"It reads that way, but all the major fences use com-mercial lines. It cuts the risk to zero."

"So you're looking at a special cargo.'

"That's affirmative." He shot a piercing glance at Bolan. "Something like a load of stolen arms."

"Speculation?"

Hannon shook his head.

"I wish it were. When I was checking out the vans, I sorted through all kinds of other theft reports—in-cluding ordnance from Camp Blanding, south of Jack-sonville, and from the naval training station at Orlando. Both within the past eight weeks."

Mack Bolan felt a tightness spreading in his gut.

"What kind of ordnance?"

"Name it. Small arms, ammunition, hand grenades and rocket launchers. Someone's sitting on enough hardware to start a private army."

"You figure some connection with the trucks?"

Hannon frowned.

"The street talk here backs it up," he said. "There's a bottomless market for arms in south Florida—ter-rorists, drug runners, exiles from all over Central America. They're buying anything that shoots."

"Okay. You're still a country mile from Tommy Drake."

"Not necessarily. I was supposed to meet with an in-formant who could put it all together, but...." He checked his watch. "Looks like I'm going to miss him."

"Just as well," the soldier told him. "If he didn't set you up himself, he may be in the bag already. If he's clear—"

"He'll get in touch," John Hannon finished for him. "Yeah, I thought of that."

They passed a small suburban shopping mall, and Bolan cut across the nearly empty parking lot, his sportster homing on a bank of pay phones next to the corner drugstore.

"This will have to do."

"It's fine. I'll have somebody here inside of five." He hesitated, halfway out the door, a frown carved deep into his honest face. And there was something going on behind his eyes.

"Your hardware... isn't that the new Beretta?"

Bolan felt the short hairs lifting on his neck. He nodded.

Hannon's frown was softening, becoming speculative.

"Fellow I used to know swore by the Luger."

Bolan forced a smile.

"It's got the power, but the toggle's too exposed," he said. "It snags."

"I guess my dope was secondhand. This fellow... well, we never really met."

There was another pregnant pause, and Bolan waited for the other shoe to drop. When Hannon spoke again, his voice was softer, cautious.

"Guess I'd better make that call," he said. He got out of the car, eyeing the phones, then he turned around to face the Executioner.

Bolan felt himself relaxing as the older man continued, smiling now.

"If I had some idea what you were looking for...."

"I'm not exactly sure myself," the soldier answered truthfully.

"Well, if there's anything...."

"I've got your number," Bolan told him.

"Mmm." No real surprise. "Well, thanks again."

He slammed the door and Bolan took the Firebird out of there, John Hannon swiftly dwindling in the rearview mirror. The P.I. had a telephone receiver in his hand, already speaking into it.

And Hannon held the fate of Bolan's mission in his hand as well. If he revealed what he suspected—what he *knew*—to the police, Miami could become a write-off. If they were expecting him—

The flash of recognition had been unavoidable, perhaps, but Hannon was a savvy war-horse, all the same. Nothing passed him by unnoticed, unexamined by the keen detective's eye. There was potential danger there, if Hannon's sense of duty forced him to report their close encounter.

But Bolan trusted the detective. Naturally. Instinctively.

A great deal more than recognition had been shared between them as they spoke. There had been understanding, yes, and something else on the detective's part.

Approval?

Grudging admiration?

Bolan frowned. If Hannon chose to play the role of ally, he might be a winning asset—or a cumbersome liability. At present, though, the Executioner had other problems on his mind.

His Miami probe was a response to rumblings in the underground, a hint of trouble dangerously near the flash point. He had bits and pieces of the puzzle, and there had been a hope that Hannon, in the private sector now, might help him put them all together. Now, instead, he had provided further riddles.

And a pointer, yes. At least that much.

He had pointed Bolan straight to Tommy Drake.

3

Tommy Drake—born Thomas Dracco—was the sole surviving son of a Chicago loan shark. Papa Dracco was "connected," but his Mob affiliations did not guarantee intelligence—nor could they save him when he sided with the loser in a local Mafia insurrection. The incumbent boss had Papa taken for a ride, and when his elder sons went looking for revenge, they disappeared without a trace.

All three of them.

And young Thomas, wiser than his siblings, suddenly acquired a taste for travel.

He had gravitated to Miami, seeking distance from Chicago. He acquired a muscle job—as Tommy Drake—with local *mafioso* Vinnie Balderone. Miami was an "open" city, filled with opportunities for someone who could follow orders. Someone who was not afraid of cracking heads and breaking legs along the way.

When Balderone went down before the Bolan guns, Drake numbly switched allegiance to the growing faction led by Nicky Fusco. Loss of relatives had taught him flexibility, and Tommy sought "adoption" in the Fusco family, taking up the duties of a first lieutenant, learning the narcotics business from a master. Later, after Nicky lost it all in yet another Bolan blitz, his protégé went shopping for a sponsor.

And discovered Don Filippo Sacco.

Tommy's penchant for adopting bosses did not signal any lack of personal ambition. On the contrary, experience had taught him to let others take the heat that came with leadership. He was content to stand in someone else's shadow, glad to profit from the fearsome reputation of his nominal superiors. They protected him while he earned them money.

No one killed the golden goose if there was any choice, and Tommy Drake was full of options. He dealt with anyone, impartially, so long as his security and profit was reasonably guaranteed.

Narcotics had been good to Tommy Drake. He prospered in the trade and became a millionaire while managing to insulate himself from the endemic mayhem that had turned Miami into the American murder capital.

The Mafia umbrella sheltered him to some extent, as did his legendary willingness to ice the competition first. For the most part he left the smaller independent operators alone, but the cocaine cowboys who encroached too readily upon his turf were fast becoming famous as endangered species.

Drugs had purchased Drake a Spanish-style estate in suburban Hollandale, an easy drive from Gulfstream Park. The likes of Frank Costello and Myer Lansky used to watch their horses run at Gulfstream, and while Tommy Drake enjoyed a fondness for the ponies, he did not aspire to ostentatious power. He remained secure within the shadows, letting others make the headlines, draw the fire.

Except shadows would not shelter Tommy Drake this night. His sanctuary was eroding, and the master dealer did not even know it yet.

Tonight the shadows served as cover for an enemy. Implacable. Determined.

And tonight, a golden goose was on the menu.

Bolan circled once around the block and found an unobtrusive parking place. His Firebird fit the neighborhood, but he did not plan to linger long enough to arouse curiosity.

A swift probe, right, with all the muscle necessary to extract some answers from his target.

The Executioner was rigged for battle as he left the Firebird. He was clad in midnight black, his face and hands already darkened with combat cosmetics. Underneath his left arm, the Beretta 98-R nestled in shoulder leather. The silver AutoMag, Big Thunder, rode the soldier's hip on military webbing, extra magazines for both handguns hung from his belt. Slit pockets in the midnight skinsuit held stilettos, strangling gear—the instruments of silent death.

A decorative wall encircled the estate. It had not been constructed with defense in mind, and Bolan scaled it easily, touching down on manicured grass inside. Across the darkened lawn, some fifty yards away, a rambling hacienda structure was ablaze with lights. As Bolan watched, a sentry moved across his field of vision, disappearing around the corner into darkness.

The warrior circled to his right and kept his back against the low retaining wall until he reached a willow grove that screened him from the house. He tugged the sleek Beretta from its sheath and eased the safety off before he moved into the trees.

His circuit brought him behind the house, and Bolan looked out on a patio complete with pool, cabanas, deep-pit barbecue. A twelve-foot-high diving tower stood at one end of the pool, and it was occupied. A lookout sat astride the diving board, a cut-down Remington 870 across his lap. From that position man and scatter-gun could cover rear approaches to the house, raise hell enough to bring the other sentries running at a sign of trouble.

The lookout had to go.

He was an obstacle, and Bolan did not have the time to work around him. He could not afford a living gunner at his back when he made entry to the hacienda proper.

Bolan thumbed his hammer back on his Beretta auto-loader. It was capable of double-action firing, but single-action gave him better first-shot accuracy. He slipped a thumb inside the 93-R's oversized trigger guard, wrapping his hand around the folding foregrip to ensure a steady shot.

He made the range at thirty yards, adjusting for the target's elevation, squeezing off a single parabellum round. The sleek Beretta's specially designed suppressor coughed, inaudible a dozen paces out, and silent death ate up the gap, boring in beneath the sentry's nose and shattering the face before it had a chance to register surprise.

The faceless man sprawled sideways off the diving board and slithered into splashdown, followed by his shotgun. His impact raised a plume of spray that pattered on the deck and diving board like summer rain, and he was gone.

But not forgotten.

Sentry number two had materialized across from Bolan, on the far side of the patio. He might have been responding to the splash or simply making rounds, but there was no way he could miss that body bobbing in the deep end. He responded automatically, hauling hardware out from underneath his jacket as he raced to poolside.

Bolan led the moving target, tracking, tightening into the squeeze. The automatic whispered twice. Down-range, his mark stumbled through an awkward pirouette, rebounding off a chaise longue in the awkward attitude of death. He came to rest against a brick retaining wall around the deep-pit barbecue.

Bolan waited in the stillness for another gunman to reveal himself. When no one surfaced after sixty seconds, he moved across the patio, aware that he was exposed beneath the outdoor floodlights.

It was a calculated risk. If there was a sniper in the darkness, the Executioner was open.

Bolan reached the back door unopposed and hesitated, reconsidering his angle of approach. With hurried strides he circled around the house, a gliding shadow homing on an ivy trellis set against the south wall.

He tested the trellis, decided it would bear his weight and scrambled nimbly upward toward the wrought-iron balcony and lighted window a dozen feet above his head. An easy step across the railing, and he stood outside the sliding windows in a pool of artificial light.

The windows were open on the balmy night, a breeze disturbing floor-length drapes. From where he stood, the Executioner could hear murmured voices beyond the curtain.

Whispering.

Cajoling.

Pleading.

The black Beretta was a cold extension of himself, and Bolan used its muzzle to divide the drapes, wide enough for him to peer through as he scrutinized the room within.

It was the master bedroom, as he had surmised from

below, and it was decorated like the set of a surrealistic porno film. Erotic "art" was plastered on the walls, and pieces of suggestive statuary were positioned here and there around the room like blind, contorted sentries.

The huge heart-shaped bed at center stage was occupied. The man and woman grappling there were unaware of Bolan's scrutiny. They never noticed as he slipped in through the drapes and moved with silent strides to stand within arm's reach of the bed.

The man was kneeling in between the woman's open thighs, his back to Bolan and the window. Overlooking one hunched shoulder, Bolan had a fragmentary picture of the woman: one firm breast, a flash of thigh, the head thrown back and angel face averted, panting.

Bolan reached out, tangling fingers of his free hand in the stud's hair, dragging his head back sharply. Kneeling on the bed, his quarry gave a startled cry, eyes swimming into focus on the autoloader leveled at his face.

"John Hannon says hello," the warrior told him softly.

And Tommy Drake was straining for an answer, getting nowhere fast. The girl came up onto an elbow, gaping at the man in black. She made no immediate attempt to hide her nudity.

"There must be some mistake," the *mafioso* said.

"You made it."

"Take it easy, pal. You'll never pull this off." A spark of hope had flared to life behind Drake's eyes. "I've got a dozen men downstairs."

"I counted two," the soldier said. "They're out of it."

The Executioner saw the man's Adam's apple bobbing as he tried to swallow.

"It's twenty questions, Tommy. Play it right, you live. If not—"

The dealer stiffened in his grasp.

"I ain't no stool."

"Okay."

Bolan drew back the hammer on the Beretta, letting Tommy hear it, balancing the silenced muzzle of his weapon on the mobster's nose. The Executioner heard a frightened little gasp from Tommy's woman and ignored it.

And his finger was already tightening on the trigger when his quarry buckled, caving in.

"Hey, now, wait a sec!" The dealer tossed a glance in the direction of his bedmate. "Can she take a walk?"

"I like her where she is."

"Okay, you call the shots."

And Tommy winced, as if his choice of words might give ideas to the man in black.

"You sent the Stomper and his bat boy after Hannon. Why?"

A heartbeat hesitation, ended by a prod from the Beretta.

"It's a private deal," the mobster said. "An outside contract."

"Who's the buyer?"

"I don't know."

The soldier frowned, released a weary sigh.

"Goodbye, Tommy."

"No, wait!"

Bolan let the automatic's muzzle dip a fraction of an inch.

"Why should I?"

"All I've got's a code name. Something for the phone, ya know?"

"You taking bids from strangers, Tommy?" Bolan did not try to hide his skepticism.

"Well, we've done some other business...this and that."

No need to press the mobster for specifics. This and that would be narcotics, Tommy's stock in trade.

"The code name," Bolan prodded.

"Huh? Oh, yeah...he goes by Jose 99." A weak attempt at laughter. "Swear to you, that's all the name I know. Those Hispanics—"

"How do you get in touch with him?"

"He gets in touch with me. Like this time...says some private dick is stepping on his action. Wants to know if I can fix it."

The Executioner said nothing. His icy gaze, the vacant stare of the Beretta, loosened the mobster's tongue.

"I told him I'd take care of it, okay? We help each other out...one hand washes the other."

Right. But no amount of scrubbing could erase the stain of blood.

"The contract's canceled," Bolan told his naked captive. "Stomper won't be coming home."

"Okay, man. Anything you say."

Too quick. Too easy.

Tommy Drake had caught a glimpse of daylight. He was running for it. Bolan kept a firm hand on the reins.

"You've got a white flag, Tommy. A reprieve. If I find out you've lied to me...."

"Hey, man, I wouldn't shine you on."

The man in black released his captive and backed away, the sleek Beretta autoloader leveled from the waist.

"Be smart," he cautioned. "You've got everything to lose."

And he was halfway to the balcony when Tommy lost it all.

The *mafioso* found his nerve, his legs, and bolted from the bed. He leaped across the prostrate woman, bounding off the mattress, breaking for a nearby nightstand. Bolan let him get there, watched him wrestle with the ornate drawer and fish around inside; he saw the flash of chrome as Tommy found his weapon.

Far enough.

The 93-R tracked across the bedroom, locking into target acquisition. The trigger yielded to a steady, gentle pressure from the forefinger, and a 9mm parabellum closed the space between them.

Tommy stumbled, sat down hard, and he was spilling scarlet from a hole beside his Adam's apple. He was struggling fruitlessly to speak, the effort forming crimson bubbles on his lips and pumping bloody streamers down across his chest. The soldier put another round between the glassy eyes and blew his carcass backward, out of frame.

The girl was on her knees and gaping at the carnage. She finally tore her eyes away from what was left of Tommy Drake and focused on Mack Bolan. There was something in her eyes, behind the shock and fear, but Bolan did not have the time to study it.

"Get dressed and shag it out of here," he said. "The party's over."

And he left her to it, exiting the way he came. The Executioner was out of numbers. It was every man now—every *person*—for himself.

His business at the Drake *estancia* was finished, right, but he had not been wholly candid with the woman. Tommy Drake was gone, but the party in Miami was not over yet. Not by a damn sight.

In his gut the soldier knew that it was only just the beginning.

4

Miami is as much a Cuban metropolis as it is American. For more than twenty years the city's heart has been Hispanic, throbbing to a Latin rhythm, crowded with the refugees of Castro's revolution. More than eight hundred thousand of them have arrived since New Year's Day of 1959—the date of Castro's final triumph in Havana.

Their arrival has transformed Miami irrevocably, for good or ill. Suburban Hialeah and Coral Gables were converted almost overnight to Spanish-speaking enclaves, but the living core of Cuban life is centered in Miami proper, in the district known as Little Havana.

Sandwiched between downtown Miami on the east and Coral Gables on the west, with Flagler Street its northern boundary and a southern demarcation line at Southwest 22nd Street, the district is a piece of Cuba physically transplanted stateside.

Billboards there are generally in Spanish, but shops with English Spoken signs dot the boulevards. The district's central artery is Southwest 8th Street, flowing one way, eastbound, over thirty blocks of shops and sidewalk coffee counters, pushcarts and corner fruit stands. Locals call the main drag Street of Gold, but the gold is long since tarnished; there is grime amid the glitter.

Frigid winds of change had battered Cuban Florida

since Bolan's visit early in his Mafia war and again some years later, and much of what was decent, warm, romantic, had been withered by the blast. Ironically, the blight had sprung from the same love of freedom that brought Cubans to Miami in the first place.

During April, 1980, half a dozen dissidents sought sanctuary at the Peruvian embassy in Havana. When the embassy officials would not give them up, Castro retaliated by withdrawing all his sentries from the compound. Within two days some seven thousand Cubans jammed the embassy, attempting to escape communism's iron-fisted rule.

Converting the embarrassment into a propaganda weapon, Castro publicly announced that anyone dissatisfied with Cuba was at liberty to leave. He opened up the port of Mariel to a rag-tag "freedom flotilla" based in South Florida. Miami exiles flocked to Mariel, attempting to collect their relatives and friends, but as they jammed the port, the Cuban leader was waiting to reveal his hole card.

Every vessel leaving Mariel with refugees aboard was forced to carry several passengers selected by the Cuban government for deportation to America. With new arrivals pouring into Florida at a rate of four thousand per day—more than one hundred twenty thousand of them by mid-June of that year—it soon became apparent that Castro was cleaning out his prisons and asylums, ridding Cuba of its undesirables by shipping them direct to the United States. If proof was needed, the statistics made it plain: within a few months of the boatlift, major crime inside Havana dropped by thirty-three percent, while metropolitan Miami showed a corresponding leap in violent felonies.

Narcotics was the booming modern industry in southern Florida, and with the cocaine cowboys came a radical increase in urban violence. A 1980 FBI report ranked six Florida cities among the nation's ten most lethal, with Miami rated first. At least a third of all the slayings in Miami's murder boom were drug related, and recent Cuban immigrants—the outcast *marielistas*—filled the local jails in mounting numbers. Soon, their names and faces were in law-enforcement record books as far away as New York, Chicago, Seattle and Las Vegas.

Backlash had been brewing in Miami, fueled by anger and frustration, seasoned with racial animosity. Gun sales were soaring, and old-line residents had started seeking safety in the suburbs, some abandoning the state entirely.

Dade County voters banned the use of public funds to encourage the use of any foreign language, burying a referendum that would make Miami an officially bilingual city.

An active fringe of anti-Castro terrorists had been adding to the violent toll in recent years with bombings, beatings and assassinations. Half a dozen groups were armed and organized at any given time, all plotting raids against the Cuban mainland, scheming toward the liberation of their homes.

Mack Bolan had enlisted in their cause at one time, welcomed the *soldados* into his own war as allies—but the times had changed for all concerned.

Today, embittered by American "abandonment" of Cuba since the missile crisis, some of the exiles saw their adopted country as the enemy. Attacks had been directed at the FBI and local law enforcement, airline offices and planes in flight, against the diplomats of nations that acknowledged Castro.

They had been linked to the assassinations of a U.S. President and a Chilean ambassador. The list was long and bloody, and it kept on growing.

Bolan knew the Cuban exiles—or he had, before the sealift—and the bitterness had poisoned everything they touched. In other days, another war, he had relied on them for assistance in the final stages of his grim Miami massacre. They had saved his life—not once, but twice—when he was wounded, cornered, and the Mafia hounds were snapping at his heels.

And one of them, the lovely Margarita, had provided Bolan with a very different kind of aid and comfort, laying down her life as a result.

The warrior owed them something, right, but circumstances altered cases. He had come to southern Florida in answer to reports of mounting terrorism, rumors of a KGB involvement somewhere. And if the exile movement that he once respected and admired had been perverted, twisted into something else....

The warrior checked himself, refusing to assume the worst. Some of the exiles had undoubtedly reverted to terrorism. Some of them might be in league with *mafiosi,* Cuban agents or the Soviets.

Some of them, right.

But in Mack Bolan's war, you did not slaughter herds of sheep to find the lurking wolf. The soldier made distinctions in selection of his targets. There were allies, enemies and bystanders—each of them indexed and filed away for handling under individual criteria.

There was no room in Bolan's everlasting war for indiscriminate attack, unreasoning response. In every combat situation certain steps were necessary for elimination of the enemy.

Penetration.

Target identification and confirmation.

Destruction.

The warrior had not yet achieved phase one of his attack plan. He possessed a code name, but without some further leads he could chase his tail around forever in Miami. He would have to find a handle on the puzzle, something. . . .

Someone in Miami knew the true identify of Jose 99. It was a simple matter of applying some strategic pressure, rattling some cages, waiting for the proper answers to fall out.

And Tommy Drake had been a starting point. His death was not the end of anything. It was the opening gun of Bolan's new Miami war, and Drake would have a lot of company in hell before the Executioner's Florida campaign was finished.

He was carrying the cleansing fire to *mafiosi,* terrorists and traitors in Miami. Someone sure as hell was going to get burned.

5

The nightmare was familiar, worn around the edges like an ancient snapshot that is taken out and handled frequently. It never varied.

There was water, dark and silky smooth, a flat obsidian plane beneath the cuticle of moon. The boat was sleek and fast despite its load of canvas-covered crates. The pilot handled her expertly, threading in and out among the Keys, running without lights for fear of Prohibition agents.

And the dreamer rode up front, as always, Thompson submachine gun tucked beneath his arm. He tasted the salty spray and smelled the marshy soil of the surrounding hummocks.

They were almost there. Another hundred yards would see them to the drop, then they could ditch the cargo. Rum and whiskey, loaded on the Cuban docks, would bring tremendous profits in the gin mills of Miami. Cut and bottled under phony labels, twenty dollars' worth of rum could easily return a grand to the investor. All you had to do was make the drop on time, avoiding any interference.

Hence the Thompson.

He had used it once, not far from here, when the reception crew had sprouted sidearms, moving in to commandeer the load. And nothing could erase the memory of strobe-light muzzle-flashes in the darkness, heavy bullets slicing through the hollow men and toppling them like stalks of grain.

It had been terrifying—and exhilarating.

He was waiting, hoping for another chance to try his hand.

A flashlight winking in the gloom, and now the pilot had his heading, throttling back and easing in against the battered pier. A Packard and the usual covered truck were parked at shoreside.

Handlers, taking in the line and scrambling awkwardly aboard, were already moving toward the cargo. One of them hung back, a trifle slower than the rest. There was something. . . .

As he turned an errant ray of moonlight fell on his face. The cold, familiar features still damp from the submersion, with the ragged, bloodless bullet scar across one cheek. The handler opened his mouth to speak, and seawater dribbled from between rubbery, lifeless lips.

The dreamer tried to lift his Thompson, found it leaden in his lifeless arms. He squeezed the trigger, but the frozen firing mechanism mocked him and the creature had him now. Its clammy fingers locked around his biceps, lifting him and shaking, shaking. . . .

Someone was shaking him awake and into hazy semiconsciousness. He twisted, recoiling violently from the hand upon his shoulder, biting off a startled scream as he recognized the houseman, Solly Cusamano.

Philip Sacco sat up in the king-size bed and brushed the hand away.

"I'm sorry boss. I hate to wake you." Solly's voice was tight, anxious.

"What the hell time is it?"

"Quarter to four."

"In the morning? This better be good, Solly."

The housecock shuffled back a pace as Sacco scrambled out of bed and found his robe.

"I didn't want to wake you," Solly said again, "but I couldn't take the chance. You never know about these guys."

"What guys?" The mobster felt his irritation mounting, and he let it show.

"You got a visitor downstairs. He's waiting in the library. Says his name's Omega."

Sacco felt a prickling of the scalp, as if his hairs were slowly standing up on end.

"What kind of name is that, for chrissakes?"

"Well, he gave me this."

A card materialized in Solly's hand and he was offering it to Sacco, holding it between his thumb and index finger as if fearing further contact might contaminate him.

Sacco stared at it, recognizing it for what it was, reluctantly accepting it from Cusamano. It was fashioned like a playing card, but smaller, and the symbol printed on its face was staring back at Sacco like a solitary, disembodied eye.

It was an ace of spades.

The death card.

Symbol of the Mafia's own elite gestapo.

In the old days when the Talifero brothers, Pat and Mike, were alive and operating from the New York headshed, the black aces were a law unto themselves within the closed fraternity of Mafia. They answered only to the brothers, and the brothers answered only to *La Commissione*.

It had been said that Pat and Mike, or any of their lethal emissaries, had the power to ice a *capo* on their own initiative, providing they could justify it later to the mob's commissioners. And they had used that sweeping power once, to Sacco's knowledge, right there in the open city of Miami.

That had been while Mack The Bastard Bolan was in town and kicking holy shit out of the brotherhood. A lot had changed since then, and little of it for the better, but the aces had been hardest hit of all. They were in flux, their status vague and ill-defined. Almost certainly, their sweeping powers had been radically curtailed. And yet. . . .

You never know about these guys.

Damn right.

"He give you any idea what he wants?"

The houseman shook his head.

"Just said he needs to see you. Right away."

"Let's go see him, then. I wouldn't want to keep him waiting."

Solly trailed him out along the landing, down the curving staircase to the first-floor library and den. A sentry was on station at the door. He nodded curtly at a sign from Cusamano, stood aside to let them enter.

Sacco's uninvited visitor was standing with his back toward the door, examining a shelf of first editions. He did not turn immediately, although he must have heard them enter, and the *capo* took the opportunity to look him over.

He was tall, broad shouldered, with dark hair and an athlete's body. He was wearing an expensive suit, the tailored jacket cut to give him room for undercover hardware.

"What's this all about?"

The stranger turned to face them. Despite the hour, he was wearing sunglasses, his eyes invisible behind the lenses. The face was ageless, etched in stone.

A gravestone, right.

"It's all about your life, Phil. Want to save it?"

Phil? The bastard had an overdose of nerve.

"We know each other?"

"I know you," the stranger said. "I know you've got a major problem on your hands."

"That so? I musta missed it."

"Heard from Tommy Drake tonight?"

The *capo* frowned. That goddammed prickling of the scalp again.

"I haven't heard from anyone tonight," he answered. "Everyone I know's asleep right now."

"I'll give you odds that Tommy won't be waking up."

The *mafioso* stiffened as an icy finger traced his spine. His fists were tightly clenched inside the pockets of his robe. He turned to Solly Cusamano.

"Get Tommy on the phone."

The houseman hesitated, glancing back and forth from Sacco to the ace.

"Hey, boss—"

"Go on," he snapped. "I'm covered here."

"Okay."

When they were alone, the *mafioso* moved to pour himself a drink, sipping it and deliberately ignoring the intruder, waiting for the liquid warmth to drive away his inner chill.

"You're wasting time," Omega told him. "And you haven't got a lot to spare."

"I'll take the chance."

Omega smiled and settled on the edge of Sacco's spacious hand-carved desk. Another silent moment passed before the houseman made his reappearance. Sacco raised an eyebrow.

"Well?"

"No answer. Want me to keep trying?"

Sacco thought about it, shook his head.

"I want somebody over there. Take care of it."

As he left, Cusamano spared another parting glance at the intruder. Phil Sacco waited for the door to close before he spoke.

"You sure?"

Omega nodded. "So are you."

"All right. So what's the story? Who's behind it?"

"You should know."

He stiffened, biting off the first obscene retort that came to mind.

"I give my people room to breathe. They handle any trouble on their own."

The ace responded with a crooked smile.

"I wouldn't say that Tommy Drake was handling it. He isn't even breathing."

The *capo* did not have an answer and Omega was not waiting for one.

"We've been hearing you've got problems with the Cubans."

Sacco snorted, downed another swallow of his whiskey.

"Everyone's got problems with the Cubans. I can handle it."

"We hope so."

We? A look of puzzlement appeared on Sacco's face.

Omega did not leave him guessing.

"You've got friends on the commission, Phil. They're concerned about your welfare. Most of them would like to see you pull it out."

Most of them, right. The *mafioso* knew a few old bastards in New York who would love to see him take a fall. Uh-huh. A few of them would dance around his casket when he bought the farm.

But Philip Sacco was not buying anything just yet.

"You tell my friends up north that everything is fine."

"They want a sign," the ace informed him.

"They'll have one," Sacco answered flatly.

"Good." Omega slithered off the corner of his desk and moved in the direction of the door. He reached it, hesitated with his hand upon the doorknob. "You ever deal with termites, Phil?"

Sacco frowned.

"Can't say I have."

Omega shook his head reflectively.

"They get inside a house like this, you never see them till it's too damn late. There's only one way to get rid of them for sure."

"Oh, yeah?"

"You torch the house, smash the ones that try to make a break. Kill everything that moves and start all over, fresh." He paused, regarding Sacco from behind the shades. "I hope you don't have termites, Phil."

"I can handle things at this end," Sacco said again, and he despised the sudden tremor in his voice.

"Okay." The door was open now; the ace was halfway through it. "You might start off with Jose 99."

The *capo* arched an eyebrow.

"What the hell is that? Some kind of Cuban beer?"

Omega laughed, and Sacco felt the color rising in his cheeks.

"I like a sense of humor," the stranger told him, growing serious again within an instant. "Check it out, Phil. Find out what your boy was doing with his breathing room. Don't let the termites bring your house down."

Philip Sacco clenched his teeth.

"I'm good at pest control," he told the closing door. If the intruder heard him, he gave no sign.

And in Omega's absence, Sacco willed his muscles to relax, returning to the wet bar for another whiskey. Too damned early to be drinking, but hell, it wasn't every day an ace dropped by to threaten you and everything you had.

And it *was* a threat. All that talk about his friends up north, the Cubans, termites in the walls—he read it loud and clear.

Sacco had a budding revolution on his hands, and Tommy Drake was probably the first in line to fall. New York knew all about it—or enough, at any rate, to send their bloodhound sniffing—and the fact of Sacco's obvious ignorance marked him as a careless *capo*, one who might be easily unseated.

Well, the bastards had a fat surprise in store for them if they believed Miami would be easy pickings. Tommy Drake had bitten off a wad he could not chew, but Sacco had the muscle to avenge his first lieutenant.

He would find out what the hell was going on—among the Cubans or the Haitians, in his own damn family if it came to that—and he would put his foot down. Right on someone's throat.

As for this Jose 99—he might be anybody. That was fine with Philip Sacco. He was smart enough and strong enough to root out anyone in southern Florida. It was a relatively simple job of pulling strings and pushing proper buttons.

Right.

And you could can that crap about an open city in Miami. All it meant for Sacco was an open grave.

His "friends" up north were looking for a sign? Okay. Sacco had one ready for them.

It would read No Trespassing.

And anyone who crossed the boundary uninvited would be leaving in a body bag.

6

Mack Bolan—alias Omega—parked his rental car outside the storm fence of the medium-security detention camp. It was early yet for visitors, and Bolan knew the other vehicles in the parking lot would all belong to prison personnel. His four-door Dodge, the Firebird's temporary stand-in, made a perfect match for all the other family sedans around him.

As the vehicle had changed, so had Mack Bolan. He no longer wore the custom-tailored suit expected of a Mafia ace. Instead, a cheaper model, clearly purchased off the rack, would help him merge with lawmen who had seen more hours than income on the job. The only constant was his sleek Beretta automatic, minus its suppressor, tucked away in leather underneath his arm.

The warrior was a master of role camouflage, adept at changing his identity without elaborate disguise. Experience had taught him that the human mind most often saw what was expected, ordinary. The art of observation was neglected, often totally ignored.

The persona of a black ace was ideal for Bolan—shrouded as the Mafia's gestapo was in mystery, invested as it was with such a fearsome reputation that the doubters seldom voiced their questions openly. "Omega" had been serving him from early in his war against the Mob, and he had served to rattle Philip Sacco—but for now, another face was needed.

Exit one Omega.

Enter Frank LaMancha, federal officer.

Bolan moved along a barbed-wire runway, mounting steps to enter the encampment's small reception building. At the desk, a beefy sergeant looked up from the newspaper he was reading, frowning at the new arrival.

"Early," he remarked. "No visitors till one o'clock."

Bolan kept it deadpan, slid his wallet with the fake ID across the desk top.

"I'm here to see Antonio Esparza."

"Nobody told me anything about it," the sergeant said irritably.

"Why don't you check it out? I haven't got all day."

A spark of anger in the washed-out eyes, and there was color rising in the oval face. A massive hand searched briefly for the telephone and found it.

"Hold your water, buddy. This could take a while."

The sergeant's call produced a neatly pressed lieutenant who examined Bolan's papers, finally returning them.

"We usually get a call," the slim lieutenant said.

"It came up overnight, but if you wanna check it out—"

The watch commander hesitated, finally shook his head.

"Guess not. What is it you want from Toro, anyway?"

"We're checking out his group for terrorist connections interstate. My boss thinks we can turn him."

The lieutenant chuckled to himself.

"Good luck. The bastard's hard as nails."

Bolan followed the lieutenant through a set of double gates and down a narrow corridor. A guard and more iron gates were waiting for them at the other end.

"You packing?" the lieutenant asked.

Bolan nodded, slipped the spare Detective Special from its holster on his belt and handed it across. The gate man locked it in his desk; they did not search Bolan for any other weapons.

They walked through the final gates and out across a kind of grassy courtyard ringed by prison buildings. Bolan recognized the mess hall, laundry, workshops. Barracks ranged behind the central buildings and beyond them, men in faded uniforms were working in the cultivated fields, observed by mounted guards.

He followed the lieutenant to a squarish blockhouse, and they went inside. The sterile lobby, with more small rooms opening on either side, revealed it as the visitation building. The lieutenant flagged a guard and issued curt instructions.

"Bring up Esparza, number 41577."

"Yessir."

Bolan trailed his guide into the nearest conference room, finished with a simple wooden table and a pair of folding chairs.

"They'll bring him up directly," the lieutenant said. "And if there's anything you need—"

"Just Toro," Bolan told him. "And some privacy."

A few minutes later a shadow filled the narrow doorway. Bolan's chair scraped concrete as he rose and turned to face the man he knew as Toro.

Time had changed Antonio Esparza, lined his face around the mouth and eyes, but Bolan recognized him instantly. The hair was still jet black, the eyes still level, hard, the jaw still firm. In prison whites, the olive of Esparza's skin appeared to be a deep suntan.

And the man still moved like the commander he had

been, with back straight, shoulders squared. The prison had not broken him; it never would, no more than Castro's jails had broken him in younger days.

El Toro was a fighter. *Hard as nails,* the young lieutenant said. Damn right.

But there was something new about the man that Bolan had not seen before. An edge of bitterness, perhaps. An anger simmering in the cauldron of his soul.

The Executioner offered him a hand and Toro brushed on past him, homing on an empty chair across the narrow table from him. Bolan nodded at an escort guard and he retreated, locked the door behind him, leaving them alone. Bolan sat down opposite the Cuban, watching him in silence for a moment prior to speaking.

"Do they bug these rooms?" he asked.

The Cuban raised an eyebrow, finally shook his head.

"No more. The civil-liberties attorneys threaten lawsuits."

Bolan took a chance.

"It's been a long time, Toro."

His companion's face was changing, melting into a reflective frown, his dark brows knitting. He was studying the Executioner, examining the altered face that he had never seen, as if to look behind the flesh and into Bolan's mind. Another moment, and the Cuban seemed to come to some conclusion.

"A face may change," he said at last, "but not the eyes, the soul. I hear that you are dead."

The warrior grinned, beginning to relax a fraction.

"That's a small exaggeration. Maybe wishful thinking."

"And the war?"

"Today it's in Miami."

"It was always here."

The soldier nodded, glanced around at their surroundings.

"Hard to carry off the fight from here. What happened?"

Bolan knew the answers, or a part of it, but he was interested in Toro's version.

"Someone says I have explosives, guns."

"I see."

The Cuban frowned.

"You do not ask?"

"No need to."

Toro shook his head disgustedly.

"It is ironic, no? For years I handle weapons, smuggle refugees, strike blows for *Cuba libre*. Now, they say I hide explosives in my home, where any fool can find them. *Está loco*."

"Someone set you up."

The Cuban spread his hands.

"*Como no*. Policemen come with warrants in the night. They know exactly where to look and what they may expect to find."

"You have a candidate?"

The freedom fighter's smile was unexpected and disarming.

"There is someone I suspect," he answered vaguely. "Ten months, perhaps a year, and I will visit him."

"You may not have the time to spare."

The Cuban studied Bolan, frowning, finally rocked back in his metal folding chair.

"Explain."

The soldier gave it to him, fragmentary as it was—the

stolen trucks and arms, the rumbles of a Cuban exile tie-in with the Mafia drug machine, and the attempt upon John Hannon. When he finished laying out the scrambled jigsaw pieces, Bolan waited, hoping that the Cuban might be able to make sense of them, provide him with a handle.

Toro's words were not encouraging.

"This Jose 99, he might belong to anyone. Your friend—the captain—is he certain his informer was a Cuban?"

The warrior nodded.

"Sure as he can be. They never met."

El Toro leaned across the table, lowering his voice conspiratorially.

"You have to understand, *amigo*...the intrigue...it has become a way of life...a cause unto itself. For twenty years, we fight to free our homeland. First, your government supports us—then it tells us to be patient, wait until *mañana*. The CIA recruits our people, trains them...and it introduces them to leaders of the Mafia. Then come the *marielistas* and their drugs...."

Bolan felt him winding down.

"I need a handle, Toro. Anything at all."

The Cuban hesitated, finally spoke.

"There may be something I can do," he said. "But from in here...."

His shrug was eloquent, and Bolan got the message. Loud and clear. He scanned the possibilities in something like a second flat, arriving at a swift decision.

"We can work it out," he said.

7

John Hannon set the telephone receiver down and kept his hand on top of it, as if to keep it from escaping. Or to keep his hand from trembling. He had been expecting anything, but even so the deep familiar voice had sent a tremor down his spine.

It was a voice from somewhere out beyond the rim of Hell.

A warrior's voice.

There had been doubts, despite the blood-and-thunder meeting that had saved his life, but Hannon was not doubting now. He was convinced beyond the shadow of a doubt.

He had just been talking to a dead man.

Hannon had pursued the soldier's holy war in the urban jungle of Miami. He had followed the commando's hellfire course across a continent and back again, until the fiery climax on a sodden afternoon in New York's Central Park.

The former captain of detectives had expected some reaction, anything—except the sudden sense of loss.

The soldier's death had left a void behind...in Hannon.

But the soldier was not dead in faraway New York. He was alive and fighting in Miami. Fighting, very probably, for life itself.

And for what else?

The morning call had been abbreviated, cryptic. The warrior had dropped a code name, listened stoically as Hannon came up empty, promised he would keep in touch.

Oh, yes. John Hannon had no doubt on that score.

In the meantime, all he had to do was trace a faceless Cuban hiding somewhere in Miami or environs, pinpoint his location, set him up—for what?

He frowned. No doubt on that score, either.

This commando was not known for taking prisoners.

Hannon pushed the morbid thought away. The war had come to him; he had not sought it out, but once involved, there was a single course available. The captain of detectives would continue until he caught a glimpse of daylight at the other end or hostiles stopped him dead.

Right now his limited objective was a Cuban stoolie known as Jose 99. And finding him could be a problem, unless. . . .

He lifted the telephone receiver, punched a number up from memory, identified himself and waited while the patch was made. Another moment and a second strong familiar voice addressed him.

"Morning, John. How are you?"

"Hanging on. Taking it easy."

"That's a good way to take it," Captain Robert Wilson told him earnestly.

It was apparent Wilson would have liked to ask him more about last night's fiasco. Hannon had worked long enough with Wilson out of homicide division to interpret tones, inflections in his voice. His was a homicide detective first and foremost, but he was also Hannon's closest friend.

"I need a favor, Bob."

"So, shoot."

"I'm looking for a Cuban, and he may be in your files. I've only got a street name."

"Yeah?"

"He goes by Jose 99. It isn't much, I know. . . ."

Suspicion crept into the homicide detective's voice. "Would this have anything to do with last night's shoot-up?"

Hannon hated lying to his friend, but it was unavoidable. He tried to sound sincere.

"It's unrelated. I've been working on a skip-trace and I'm getting nowhere fast."

"I see." The skepticism carried in his voice across the wire. "I'll run it through, but don't expect too much."

"Appreciate it. Listen, Bob, I wish I could help you with this other thing."

"Well, if you don't have any information. . . ."

Wilson left the statement dangling, giving him a chance to spill, but Hannon held his peace.

"You know if there was anything at all I'd let you in on it."

"I hope so, John."

And there was something very much like sadness in Bob Wilson's voice.

"If you come up with anything on this Jose. . . ."

"I'll call you," Wilson told him. "In the meantime, why not take some time off? Get yourself some rest."

"I'm way ahead of you. Just have to clear a few things up before I take the time."

"Uh-huh. John?"

"Yeah?"

"Watch your ass."

The former captain of detectives smiled.

"I always do."

BOB WILSON ROCKED BACK in his swivel chair and glowered at the silent telephone. He felt an urge to call John Hannon back, but dismissed it. There was no time for playing wet nurse, not with metropolitan Miami in the middle of a sizzling crime wave. Manila folders piled on his desk bore mute testimony to the work load facing Homicide these days.

It used to be John Hannon's desk...John Hannon's office. Wilson owed the older man a lot, he realized. The former captain of detectives taught him most of what he knew about survival on the streets—the things they never mentioned in police academies. And Hannon literally saved his life on one occasion. Yes, there could be no forgetting that.

They had been working on a string of hooker killings that made Jack the Ripper look humane. The evidence was slim, but through a string of lucky breaks they had finally narrowed the field to one substantial suspect: big and bad, a six-time loser, psychopathic woman hater with a string of brutal incidents behind him. Rumors on the street said he had taken up the knife to do a little twisted civic renovation on his own.

They had traced him to a seedy rooming house and Hannon took the front, with Wilson riding shotgun, uniforms staked out to cover the retreats. Before they had a chance to reach the subject's room, he met them on the dingy, narrow stairs, a psycho's sixth sense warning him of danger, driving him to the attack.

The memories of that desperate battle in the darkness

still made Wilson queasy. He had been moving up the stairs, a step ahead of Hannon, when a snarling human monster loomed ahead of him, airborne. Talon-fingers had locked around Wilson's windpipe, and the butcher knife was flashing toward his face when Hannon's roaring Magnum brought the curtain down.

So he owed John Hannon, right. He worried when the old man courted danger. Not that Hannon could not pull his weight, but this time his ass was hanging out a mile. He was dabbling in some deadly business now, and never mind the crap about some hoodlums trying to avenge an old arrest. Bob Wilson was not buying that one for a second, and if Hannon had been lying to him, there must be something he was bent on hiding.

Now this Cuban thing—what was it? Jose 99. A street name, sure, designed to hide the true identify of someone who was dealing weapons, drugs, or simple information. Any one of those commodities could get you butchered in a hurry.

The Cuban scene these days was lethal. Sprinkle in the Haitians and Colombians, a hefty dash of coke and heroine, and start the blender. What came out the other end was sudden death, and there were bodies filling up the county morgue to prove it.

Hannon could get blown away without even trying. All he had to do was ask the wrong question—or the right one, of the wrong person. He could wind up in a gutter or feeding 'gators in the Everglades. It happened every day around Miami.

Still, he owed the captain one, and Wilson would inquire about the Cuban for him. If he stumbled over something he could use along the way, well, so much the better.

He would do that much for Hannon, right. And, maybe, with a little luck, he could preserve a friend's life in the process. Maybe.

8

"We're almost there."

The pilot had to raise his voice to make it heard above the helicopter's engine. In the seat beside him, Bolan did not need to check his watch; he knew they were on time. Soon they would reach the pickup point.

Jack Grimaldi had been bringing Bolan into hot landing zones from early in his private war against the Mafia. Reluctantly at first, and later with a convert's zeal, he had provided vital air support on some of Bolan's most demanding missions, calling on every skill as a flier to put the Executioner into striking range.

Grimaldi had survived the storm that shattered Bolan's Stony Man command center and blew away a portion of his life. The Italian-American flyboy had made a tacit avowal, then, to help the big guy—who had pointed Grimaldi on the right path—wherever the canker of evil reared its head.

Two warriors, joined in spirit, fighting for a cause.

But nothing they had ever done together matched the sheer audacity of Bolan's morning mission on the outskirts of Miami.

Grimaldi held the Bell at cruising speed a hundred feet above the highway, running parallel to northbound traffic. Fields of grassland and palmetto stretched away on either side of the two-lane blacktop.

The Executioner was dressed in camouflage fatigues and jump boots, cheeks and forehead streaked with jungle war paint. Heavy bandoliers of ammunition hung across his chest and cut into his shoulders.

Bolan's weapon of the moment was a portable artillery piece, the XM-18 semiautomatic launcher. It resembled nothing quite so much as an old-fashioned Tommy gun complete with pie-pan drum, but time had wrought some drastic changes in the formula. The smoothbore weapon chambered 40mm rounds and could deliver them with accuracy at one hundred fifty yards. An expert hand could place a dozen lethal rounds on target in the space of five seconds—anything from high explosives and incendiaries to the deadly needlelike flechettes.

But at the moment, warrior Bolan's launcher was equipped with ammunition of a different nature. Cans of smoke and tear gas alternated in the drumlike cylinder with nonlethal batton rounds, specially designed for crowd control in riot situations. While the current mix would let him blind and gag an enemy, or knock him on his ass with stunning force, it would not deal a fatal blow to any man of average health.

The Executioner was rigged for battle, right—but with a crucial difference. This time out, nobody was supposed to die. If blood was spilled, Mack Bolan did not want to be responsible.

And yet, of course, he would be.

He had already turned over the options in his mind, examined every facet. This was simply, undeniably, the only way to go.

He was breaking Toro out of prison.

It was the first time he had ever tried to liberate a

prisoner from "friendly" hands, and he was pledged to bring it off without a bloodbath. Prison guards were like police in Bolan's estimation—soldiers of the same side in his war against the savages who preyed upon a civilized society.

Their methods differed radically, and many of the men in uniform would drop him if he gave them half a chance, but soldier Bolan had preserved a unilateral ceasefire with law-enforcement officers from the beginning of his Mafia war. No matter what they did or tried to do in the performance of their duty, regardless of the strain of corruption left upon some isolated badges, Bolan would not drop the hammer on a fellow fighting man.

But the soldier was a realist. He was well aware that Toro's airlift out of prison would require some cover fire. A little something that would cause confusion, leave the guards a bit disoriented, and perhaps a little bruised.

The XM-18, with its riot loads, had solved the problem for him. If he played his hand with skill they could be in and out before the reinforcements gathered, bringing up the heavier artillery.

Mack Bolan pushed the odds out of his mind and concentrated on the countryside below. They were no longer following the highway, but a narrow asphalt ribbon sliced across the landscape off to Bolan's left. In front of them the prison compound was a tiny clutch of buildings, growing closer by the moment.

As they crossed the outer fence a mounted guard made visual contact, waving frantically to warn them off. When they ignored him, he removed a walkie-talkie from his saddle horn and started speaking rapidly into the mouthpiece.

Bolan marked the rider and dismissed him. He could never catch them now, and if they played it right, the reinforcements he was calling up would not have time or opportunity to cut them off.

It hinged on Jack Grimaldi now, and on their small remaining element of surprise. Assuming that the mounted guard had radioed direct to the command post, instead of warning personnel on duty in the fields, they had a chance.

Bolan primed the launcher, tucking it beneath his arm. He shrugged out of the safety harness, moving back to take his station in the chopper's loading bay. Below them, rows of crops flashed past beneath the Bell, almost close enough to touch.

They flew over another horseman and he wheeled around to follow them, brandishing the lever-action .30-30 that was standard issue. Convicts, scattered up and down the rows, were taking full advantage of the interruption, leaning on their hoes and shovels, watching the helicopter.

More cons below them now, more horsemen rapidly converging, driving mounts into a lather. Bolan spotted Toro in among the others. The Executioner knew Grimaldi had the Cuban now, as the bird began circling, hovering, preparing to land. The chopper's rotor wash flattened the rows of collard greens and forced men down there to shield their eyes.

They were a dozen feet from touchdown when Mack Bolan opened fire. He swung up the XM-18 and triggered three quick rounds, the belching muzzle swinging on a track from left to right. Two bursts of smoke erupted on the field, and in the midst of it a tear-gas can exploded, mingling noxious fumes with Bolan's artificial fog bank.

Grimaldi set the chopper down amid the greens, and rotor wash was working for them now, propelling clouds of smoke and gas across the field in an expanding screen.

There was mass confusion as the cons started shouting, gagging as they scattered, seeking daylight. Bolan saw a pair of riders bearing down on the helicopter, then the smoke screen cut them off from view. He lobbed another sputtering can in their direction.

Above the general din, he heard a guard attempting to bring order out of chaos, shouting at his charges, firing in the air. Off to Bolan's right another rifle cracked in answer, the bullet drilling through his smoke screen.

A mounted guard exploded into view, his animal colliding with a startled inmate, hurling him to the ground. The rider was fighting with his reins and rifle simultaneously, struggling to stay aboard and get a shot at the intruders. He was tracking onto target when the gelding made a break for cover in the smoke and dumped him off the starboard side.

He touched down hard, the .30-30 jarred out of his hand on impact.

The fallen convict scrambled toward the .30-30, retrieving it and fumbling with the lever action for a moment, finally chambering a round. Ignoring Bolan and the helicopter, he was sighting on the semiconscious guard, already tightening his finger on the trigger when the XM-18 roared.

The range was thirty feet and there was little need to aim. The hard batton projectile struck the convict underneath his arm and punched him over sideways in the dirt, his captured rifle spinning free.

A running figure cleared the smoke and Bolan recognized El Toro, sprinting for the chopper. Close behind him, three more inmates were intent on keeping pace, the nearest of them threatening to overtake him in the break for freedom.

Bolan swung his light artillery around to intercept them, but the Cuban was directly in his line of fire. To take out the leader he would have to topple Toro, and the other two were fading back now, legging it in single file to let their pointman take the heat.

The Cuban feinted left, and Bolan was about to drop his closest competition when El Toro spun around and drove a fist into the convict's sweating face. Momentum did the rest, and Toro's opposition touched down shoulders first, a tumbling rag doll.

His companions hesitated, breaking stride, and they were circling Toro in a pincer movement, Bolan and the chopper momentarily forgotten. One of them threw himself at Toro with his arms outstretched, talon fingers groping for the Cuban's windpipe.

Toro took him low and inside, catching him off balance with a slashing knee that crushed his genitals. The man doubled over, retching, and his nose was flattened by the toe of Toro's boot. He vaulted backward, unconscious before he hit the turf.

His backup was considering an angle of attack, but he never got the chance to follow through. A rifle cracked and Bolan saw the straw man airborne, pitching forward on his face beneath the deadly impact of a .30-30 slug.

The Executioner reacted swiftly, pivoting to face the source of gunfire. He spotted a prison guard some thirty paces to his right. The rifleman was seeking other targets, blind with panic now and desperate to do something, *anything,* before it was too late.

The launcher bucked and bellowed, sent another stunner out to close the gap between them. Downrange, Bolan's target hurtled backward, propelled into a sprawl by the batton round's impact. Bolan turned his full attention back to Toro, focusing upon the mission.

And his passenger was there, one arm outstretched to grasp the helping hand that Bolan offered. Jack Grimaldi saw the Cuban come aboard, and the pilot reacted instantly. The ship lifted off, ascending vertically, the altered angle of their rotor blast dispersing smoke and gas.

Below them riflemen were searching for the range and finding it. A bullet whispered next to Bolan's ear and drilled an exit port behind him, through a pane of Plexiglas. Another twanged against the fuselage and spun away.

Grimaldi took them out of there, the Bell responding to a master's hand and climbing, banking, rising in a spiral that would get them out of rifle range.

The Executioner and Toro scrambled into seats and buckled up, riding out the storm. Grimaldi soon had them running true and arrow straight above the scrublands, with the prison compound dwindling behind them.

Across from Bolan, Toro was beginning to relax, but his deliverer could not afford to share the feeling. They were flying out of momentary danger into greater peril, and the heat would follow them inexorably. The spark that he had struck that morning might ignite a lethal conflagration in Miami.

Fine.

Warrior Bolan was familiar with the heat; he thrived on it.

And he was carrying the fire this time, a cleansing flame to scorch the savages and drive them underground.

A number of his enemies had felt the Bolan heat already. More would follow. Hell had come acalling in Miami, and the purifying flames would have to run their savage course.

A skillful hand could fan the flames, attempt to channel and direct them, but the end result would be in doubt until the final shot was fired. There was every chance that warrior Bolan would be counted with the fallen, but he knew the long odds going in, and they did not deter him.

The Executioner was blitzing on.

9

Toro stood before the open kitchen window, leaning on the sink and staring out across a scruffy yard in the direction of a peeling clapboard fence. The nearest neighbor was an auto graveyard, its rusting hulks piled high above the fence.

"Sorry we couldn't set up something with a view."

Grinning, the Cuban turned to face Mack Bolan.

"The view is fine, *amigo*. I was getting tired of open spaces, anyway."

He retrieved a mug of coffee from the kitchen counter, sat down at a narrow dining table to face the Executioner.

"I have not yet thanked you for delivering me."

"No thanks are necessary," Bolan told him.

"Ah. Without the need, then. *Gracias, amigo*."

"Welcome."

They were seated in the combination dining room and kitchen of a rented bungalow in Opa-locka, a Miami suburb. It was five minutes from the Opa-locka airport and well removed from Little Havana. And Bolan knew that it was there the main heat of the coming search for Toro would be concentrated. With any luck the hunt should pass them by completely.

Not that Bolan or the Cuban planned on hiding out while the search went on around them. Far from it.

They were pausing at the rented safehouse only long enough to coordinate a course of action.

There was work to do yet in Miami, and before proceeding with it, Bolan needed information.

"You mentioned a suspected sellout in your group."

Toro glanced up from his coffee cup, a frown etched into his forehead. He hesitated, and when he spoke, his voice was solemn.

"I will deal with him myself."

"I understand your feelings."

Toro raised an eyebrow.

"Do you?"

Bolan nodded.

"Faint hearts...traitors...they injure all of us."

He did not speak of April Rose or of the mole who had done everything within his power to scuttle Bolan's Phoenix program. Good lives down the drain, and changes—driving Bolan back into the cold and giving back his name, his lonely war.

The Cuban was consumed with private thoughts, his own grim memories, but Bolan's voice cut through the fog.

"I need your help," he said. "If this connects, I can't afford to go in firing blind."

Another hesitation, then Toro finally nodded.

"Raoul Ornelas." He pronounced the name as if it left a sour taste on his tongue.

"My right-hand man. *Mi hermano.*" Disgust was heavy in his voice. "You know I worked with Alpha 66?"

Bolan nodded. The computer files at Stony Man had kept him current on a host of paramilitary groups, their personnel—anything and everything related to the

covert war of terrorism. While it lasted, he had followed
Toro's progress through the Cuban exile underground,
had been relieved when he affiliated with a moderate
faction, had seen him rise into a leadership position,
helping to direct the energies of soldiers who might
otherwise have run amok.

"Raoul, he was not satisfied. More action...always
more. He blames your government for all our problems.
FBI or CIA, they're all the same with Castro to Raoul."

The Cuban downed his coffee, then got up to refill his
mug.

"We quarreled over policy. I learned Raoul was acting independently, recruiting others. Bomb here,
there...all the same to him."

"He challenged you?"

The Cuban's eyes flashed back at him.

"I threw him out." The sudden smile was almost
wistful. "No use. There is always somewhere for a man
to go."

"Ornelas set you up?"

A casual shrug.

"Raoul, or one of his *soldados*," Toro answered.
"Before the trial, he is already meeting with my men, re-
minding them they cannot trust the government, inviting them to join him."

Bolan saw the picture clearly, all the ugly pieces falling into place.

"You know the EAC—Exiles Against Castro?"

"Yes."

The Executioner was only too familiar with the exile
splinter movement. Known to law-enforcement agencies
since 1975, EAC was a tiny clique numerically—fewer
than one hundred hard-core members had been publicly

identified—but it exerted influence beyond proportion to its numbers.

EAC drew support from leading members of the anti-Castro bloc. Successful exile businessmen supported the guerrilla band with money, arms, a well-timed word in certain ears.

And for their efforts, they got action, right.

The soldiers of EAC had been linked with bombings from Miami to Manhattan, random acts of violence and intimidation. They were indiscriminate in choosing targets: federal, state or local offices; the homes and businesses of opposition spokesmen; foreign embassies and airlines. Voices raised against the terror were silenced by the bomb or sniper's bullet, and EAC won grim recognition as the most savage, most secretive faction of the splintered Cuban exile movement.

Freedom of expression had a fearful price in southern Florida, and everyone was paying. Everyone, that is, except the Communists and *Fidelistas* whom EAC was presumably established to combat. Strangely, and despite the rising tide of Cuban violence, little of the action seemed to be directed at the classic goal of liberating Cuba from the blight of Castroism.

"Raoul is influential in the group. Some say he leads it now, except in name."

"I see."

EAC.

Weapons, trucks and drugs.

The Mafia.

A link was not beyond the realm of possibility, Bolan knew, but he needed much more in the way of solid battlefield intel before choosing targets for elimination. Nothing was precisely what it seemed among the exiles;

anything could happen, and the Executioner could not afford mistakes that might cost lives.

"What will you do?" the Cuban asked, his voice intruding on the warrior's thoughts.

"Start rattling cages," Bolan told him. "I don't have a handle yet, but somebody out there can give me one."

"Raoul?"

The Executioner shrugged. "I recognize your claim," he said. "But if you shake loose something helpful...."

Toro spread his hands.

"*Como no*. Of course. You are my friend. I owe you my freedom."

"You owe me nothing," Bolan told him solemnly. "All debts are canceled. From here on out, I can't predict where this will take me."

Toro frowned.

"You fear that it will lead you to my people. *Mis hermanos*."

"I've considered it," the Executioner admitted candidly.

"And I." The Cuban leaned across toward Bolan, and there was a sadness mixed with pain in Toro's eyes. "I understand Ornelas, his *soldados*. They have spent a lifetime fighting *Fidelistas*. First encouraged by your government, then punished."

Your government. Mack Bolan read the none-too-subtle message loud and clear. It drove the meaning home—that they were different, he and Toro. Different warriors with—perhaps—different wars to wage.

"I feel the same anger," Toro was continuing. "But even so...."

He hesitated, struggling with a problem that had clearly nagged him long and hard.

"A man must know his enemies," the Cuban said at last. "The blood, it is not enough. In here—" he tapped his chest above the heart "—a man can die before his time. A brother can betray his blood."

The Executioner was silent for a moment. When he spoke again, his tone was solemn.

"Blood doesn't always make a brother."

Toro nodded.

"*Sí. Comprendo.* I will help you... if I can."

Bolan felt the shadow pass between them once again, but briefly. He dismissed it, knowing that he could not chart the Cuban's course of action for him. He trusted Toro's instincts, his sense of honor.

Bolan rose, prepared to leave.

"I'm on the numbers, Toro. Give you a ride somewhere?"

The Cuban shook his head and nodded toward the kitchen telephone.

"I make a call," he said. "There are *soldados* still that I can trust."

"Okay. Is there someplace I can leave a message?"

Toro thought about it for an instant, finally rattled off a number from memory, and Bolan memorized it.

"I'll be in touch," he promised.

Toro rose and clasped his hand in parting, wrung it warmly.

"*Vaya con dios, amigo.*" And the Cuban's sudden smile was dazzling. "*Viva grande,* Matador."

Live large. Damn right.

The Executioner was out of there and tracking, leaving Toro to his own devices. They were separate soldiers, separate wars.

Mack Bolan hoped that they would meet again as allies, or at least as friendly neutrals. He had no wish to take the brave *soldado's* life, or risk his own in the attempt.

But he was moving now, and there could be no turning back.

Hunting.

Seeking out the savages in civilized Miami.

Rattling cages, right.

And living large.

10

The *bolita* handler shook his burlap bag filled with numbered Ping-Pong balls. He swung it twice around his head and let it fly. In the audience a planted "catcher" shouldered two smaller men aside and snatched the tumbling bag out of midair, holding it aloft and shaking it in triumph. Then he untied the bag and reached inside, drawing out one of the balls and barely glancing at it, tossing it up to the handler on the dais.

The handler made a show of staring at the ball, as if he had some difficulty reading the single digit painted on its surface. Finally he raised it between a thumb and forefinger for the small crowd to examine.

"*Nueve*. Number nine."

Down on the betting floor two or three patrons gave a halfhearted cheer; the rest stood silent or groaned softly, crumpling the numbered betting slips they held in their hands.

Three winners, maybe twenty losers. It was just about the right proportion for a crowd this size, Ernesto Vargas thought.

At thirty-six, Vargas was the boss and operator of a moderate but lucrative *bolita* territory covering Coral Gables and surrounding neighborhoods. Some three years off the boat, he was already doing better than he ever dreamed was possible in Cuba.

Connections had got him started in *bolita* and staked him to his first successful parlor—a debt that he had long ago repaid with interest.

Common sense would take him to the top in time, if he did not step on any lethal toes along the way.

Ernesto Vargas had been learning from the moment he set foot upon the mainland of America. Studying the people who had come before him, and the Anglos who were there before them all. He made a special study of the native laws and how to circumvent them with a minimum of risk.

It was simple, really. You bought a franchise from the Mob, you greased the cops...and generally speaking, you were free to operate in peace around south Florida, as long as you did not attract undue attention to yourself.

Ernesto Vargas knew the art of living inconspicuously. He might be known within Coral Gables as the man to see for certain favors, but his name had not been splashed across the headlines like the goddamned cocaine cowboys with their fast cars and machine guns, killing people in the streets like rabid dogs.

If Vargas needed someone taken care of...perhaps roughed up a little, or perhaps a lot...he took care of it privately, without the fanfare that attended so much of Miami's recent violence. A kneecap here, an elbow dislocated there. His debtors paid, for the most part on time, and life went on.

It was the American dream.

He had already learned to screw the peasants on *bolita* and the Cuban lottery he dabbled in, nickel and diming them out of a cool one hundred thousand a year. Not bad for an ex-convict who had been loaded on a boat at gunpoint, in Mariel harbor, not so long ago.

Seated on the dais, back behind his handlers, Vargas scanned the little crowd of players. It was daylight yet, with hours to go before the darkness brought the real money in, but for a morning shift the crowd was far from disappointing. With any luck at all, Vargas would clear an easy grand before lunchtime, half for himself, the rest divided up between his handlers, catchers and the muscle he maintained at every game to watch for trouble.

They were meeting in a private dwelling, one of half a dozen Vargas rented for his floating games. He rotated locations on a regular schedule, helping the Vice cops save face, keeping up the charade. For their trouble and the inconvenience of having strangers, often drunks, arrive and gamble in their homes, the actual tenants made a hundred dollars daily.

It was cheap insurance, a damn sight cheaper than his pad with the local sheriff's department. If there had been a way to eliminate the cops and politicians with their hands out, Vargas was convinced he could rake off another twenty-five percent of gross each month to keep for himself and to invest in other projects.

He dismissed the thought, half smiling to himself. The system had existed for two centuries, and it resisted the way a slab of granite stood against the wind and rain. In time, it might be altered, but to observe the changes in a single lifetime....

The handler was shaking his bag again, and bets were going down around the room. The writers were working quickly, pretending the handler was likely to throw before they had a chance to siphon every nickel from the audience. The all-male audience was noisy now, each man calling out his bets, some of them digging deeper for the cash than they had earlier, but still coming up with it just this one time.

And the next time, right. And the next.

Vargas knew his people, knew they loved *bolita* and the lottery the way black people were supposed to love the numbers, or the rich old Jewesses their slot machines up north, around Atlantic City.

Everybody gambled, and the fact that it might be against the law would never alter human nature. In the back of his mind Ernesto Vargas saw himself as part of some great public service, giving men and women what they wanted, something that the heartless politicians had decreed was out of bounds.

He was a hero, right. A man of his community, of the people.

The handler swung his bag overhead, released it, aiming with precision at a different catcher, salted in another corner of the room. Vargas watched the burlap sack as it was airborne, tumbling gracelessly, a dark misshapen blur against the backdrop of the parlor windows.

Windows that were suddenly imploding, collapsing inward in a shower of fractured glass. Someone screamed, then everyone was babbling at once, turning to gape at the windows.

The catcher was turning with them, missing the bag and never really noticing as it struck him on the shoulder and tumbled to the floor. Its ties became unfastened, and the numbered balls were spilling everywhere—all except unlucky thirteen, fastened to the burlap with a tiny patch of Velcro for the catcher's convenience.

A wasted play now, but Ernesto Vargas had his mind on other things, momentarily forgetting lost profits as he stood up, kicking over his folding metal chair and shouldering past his handlers toward the front of the dais.

"What the—"

And he saw an oval object in the middle of the parlor floor, still spinning from the force of impact, spewing colored smoke now in a blinding cloud. The bettors were scattering away from the grenade, seeking out the available exits as they ran. Some of them were dropping money all along the way, and Vargas made a mental note to pick it up as soon as he could get a handle on exactly what the hell was happening.

It could not be police, he was confident of that. They had been greased, and anyway, they always called ahead. Whenever it was necessary to sacrifice a game for the sake of appearances, Vice made certain that Ernesto was not in, and that the lion's share of his daily take was safely evacuated before they rolled in, arresting handlers and bettors on various misdemeanor charges.

No, it would not be the cops.

But who?

A burst of automatic fire erupted from the direction of the home's adjacent kitchen. There was a sudden scream, cut off abruptly, and Vargas imagined that he recognized the voice of his back-door lookout, Esteban.

He saw his gunners, Ramon and Paco, moving fast in that direction, digging at the handguns they wore underneath their jackets. They were young and quick, and whoever had the frigging nerve to crash this party would regret the day that he had met them.

Vargas circled, putting the wooden podium between him and the kitchen doorway, sliding one hand down in the direction of the pistol that he carried in his belt. Ramon and Paco were almost to the door when it burst open, to reveal a tall dark figure dressed in camouflage fatigues, a smoking Uzi submachine gun in his hands.

The gunners peeled off to either side but the intruder was faster, and his weapon cut a blistering arc across the smoky room.

Vargas saw Ramon and Paco twisting, pummeled by the stream of 9mm parabellum rounds. Neither one of them got off a shot before he died, and now the master of *bolita* in Coral Gables was alone.

He took a breath and, half gagging on the smoke, made his move. The commando saw it coming, pivoted, and stroked another short burst from the Uzi. The podium took most of it, but Vargas caught a bullet in his shoulder, then another in the hip, spinning him around like a blow from some giant fist, dumping him facedown upon the dais.

His gun was gone, consciousness fading fast. He felt the rough hand on his shoulder now, turning him over onto his back. He clenched his teeth against the pain but made no sound beyond a whimper.

The barrel of the Uzi was inches from his face, and he could feel its heat, see little tendrils of smoke curling up from the flat, staring eye.

The gunner loomed above him like a giant in the colored, swirling smoke, bending over and speaking softly, barely loud enough for Vargas to make out his words.

"I'm back. Somebody knows why. Spread the word."

Something dropped onto Vargas's chest, making him flinch and close his eyes, ready for death, but when he opened them a moment later, he was all alone.

Alone with the dead.

Straining, fighting off the pain from his shoulder, he craned his neck and glanced down, squinting at the object glittering on his bloodstained shirtfront, trying to make recognition through the haze that fogged his mind.

And in an instant Vargas knew precisely what it was, although he could not hope to grasp its meaning.

The object on his chest was a marksman's medal.

LeRoy Withers—alias Mustaffa ben-Keladi—lounged behind a battered desk in his back-room office of the Club Uhuru. He studied the briefcase on his desk top as he cracked his knuckles nervously.

He was waiting for a man that he had never seen before to take the satchel off his hands. . . and to leave something else in return.

The Club Uhuru was closed and one of his men was positioned out front to meet the contact when he showed. Another gun was close by Withers, in the office—just in case.

A guy had to be careful these days, he mused, what with all that bad shit going down in Miami. It was getting so that businessmen could not conduct their deals without an escort any more. As a man with many deals in progress, he had much to fear.

The hit on Tommy Drake had been a shock, but Withers was used to rolling with the punches as they came. He learned that early, growing up on ghetto streets, and he had been an avid student of survival. There were new connections everywhere, and it had not taken long to find a new supplier.

Not long at all.

In fact the hit on Drake might wind up being good for business—at least for his own business. A resourceful man could move up quickly in a vacuum, and LeRoy had been considering for some time now that all that Cosa Nostra crap had outlived its usefulness. It might be time for a righteous brother to assert himself, kick some ass and bring in the respect he had deserved for so damned long.

Of course, he would have to show a little style along the way. A little steel and muscle, if it came to that.

And LeRoy Withers knew that he was equal to the task.

A sharp knock sounded on the office door. Beside him, LeRoy's man slid a hand inside his velvet jacket, finding iron beneath his arm. Satisfied, Withers kicked back in his swivel chair.

"In!"

The door swung open to admit a tall white dude, decked out in sharp expensive threads, aviator's shades and carrying a briefcase.

LeRoy grinned.

And the grin became a beaming smile as he thought about exactly what the white man would have inside that briefcase, bagged and ready for him. "Snow" in the middle of summer, damned right.

"What is it, my man?"

"It's business," the stranger replied, unsmiling, and Withers reflected once again that whites seemed not to have a sense of humor.

The new arrival placed his case on top of Withers's desk, then glanced around, found LeRoy's backup watching from the open office doorway with his hand braced on a hip, six inches from gun leather.

"You got what I need, man?" LeRoy asked him.

And LeRoy noticed for the first time since the dude entered the office, he smiled—a chilling, icy grimace.

"Right here," he replied.

The briefcase latches sounded like explosive charges shattering the stillness of the room. The lid was up, the dude was reaching inside—and LeRoy craned his neck, anxious for a look at the cocaine that he had bargained for by phone but had not sampled yet.

Perhaps a couple of snorts, just to make certain it was good enough for his high-priced clientele.

But no white powder, no plastic bag emerged from the briefcase. Instead, the man was brandishing a long silver handgun, looking better than a foot long as it hung there, a yard from LeRoy's face. He gaped at it for what seemed like a lifetime, but in fact mere seconds passed before the still life burst into explosive action.

The tall stranger swiveled, reaching out with his blaster and almost touching the muzzle to the nearest gunner's cheek before he pulled the trigger. A thunderous explosion echoed through the Club Uhuru, and the gunner's face and head disintegrated, dispatching tiny fragments all over the room. His headless body tumbled backward, hitting the floor with a resounding thud.

Beyond the door, LeRoy's other backup gun was already digging for hardware, backpedaling and looking for cover. The cannon roared again, lifting him off his feet, the force of one heavy round impacting on his chest, hurling him back several yards. He touched down by the empty bar with a single twitch before he came to final rest.

LeRoy was wearing a pistol in his belt, with another in the desk drawer for emergencies like this. Except there had never been such an incident, and in the panic of the moment he could think of only one thing.

Survival.

Clearly, drawing down on this bad-ass dude was certain suicide. And Withers was not feeling suicidal. Not in the least.

The cannon's muzzle was directly in his face now, looking larger than an oil drum at point-blank range. Withers half imagined he could crawl inside it if he tried, and hide there from the man who plainly meant to kill him.

But the gunner did not fire. Instead he fished around inside a pocket of his flashy jacket, coming out with something small and silver, which he dropped in the middle of LeRoy's cluttered desk top.

"Spread the word," the man growled, his voice graveyard cold. "I'm back. Somebody knows why."

And LeRoy watched him retreat out of there with the satchel—LeRoy's goddamned satchel full of twenties and fifties—the blaster never wavering off its kill zone as he cleared the doorway, backing right across the club room on his way to the exit.

Withers kept his eyes riveted on that pistol until the dude was out of there and clear. He made no move to follow, never seriously considering going after him and trying to retrieve the cash.

LeRoy glanced around at the wasted bodies of his soldiers, then down at the spreading moisture in the crotch of his own maroon slacks.

Some damn fine mess, yeah. Hell! But he was alive, still kicking, and now his job would be to stay that way. His hand was shaking as he reached for the telephone and started dialing.

Spreading the word.

11

The ten-year-old Cadillac cruised slowly eastward along Eighth Avenue. The driver kept a careful eye on other motorists and the flow of erratic pedestrians around him, while his three companions took in every detail of the boulevard.

Eighth Avenue.

The locals called it *Calle Ocho,* and it ran right through the heart of Miami's Little Havana district. It was the artery that fed the Cuban community's pulsing heart, alive with color, sound and movement.

The Cadillac rolled slowly down the avenue, the four occupants inspecting sidewalks jammed with cigar-chomping men in their crisp *guayaberas*—the white cotton shirts of the tropics—and women in bright-colored skirts and blouses. The street was lined with shops and family businesses: boutiques and factories where under-paid employees rolled cigars by hand; sidewalk counters selling aromatic Cuban coffee and *churros*, long spirals of deep-fried sweet dough.

They passed the Bay of Pigs monument, standing tall and proud in Cuban Memorial Plaza, and one of the men in the back seat crossed himself, muttering a hasty benediction. In the front seat, riding shotgun, his companion merely frowned and looked away.

It was so long ago, so many years and wasted lives,

but still the memory was sharp, painful. He wondered if it ever would recede, give up its power to bring a lump into his throat.

Someday, perhaps. When all the debts were canceled out, repaid in full.

Someday.

But not this day.

They turned off *Calle Ocho* into a residential side street, rolling along past neatly kept houses, many of them with shrines on the lawns, devoted to Saint Lazarus.

Only a parable now to the Catholic church, Lazarus was a living hero to the exiles for his ability to persevere through poverty and pain. They saw themselves in Lazarus—and shared the hope that broken lives might one day be revived in *Cuba libre*. Saint Lazarus was the living symbol of rebirth, of the human spirit's stubborn refusal to stay down.

A few more blocks, the houses smaller now, devoid of shrines, still neat but no longer picturesque. Beside the driver, Toro scanned the houses, searching for a number, finally picking out the one he sought.

A curt instruction to the driver, and they cruised past the target house, not even slowing. Nothing in their posture would have told a watcher that the men were hunting, and that they had found their prey upon this quiet street.

The driver took a right at the next intersection, parking out of sight and killing the engine. They unloaded, Toro taking time to readjust the pistol in his waistband, waiting for the others to form a tight semicircle at the curb. The four men were alert, trying to watch every direction at once, as if expecting an ambush on this placid residential boulevard.

In recent years the Cuban community had become fragmented, different factions violently at odds. Little Havana had assumed the atmosphere of a city under siege—but from within. There was no enemy outside the gates; the city's people had engaged each other in a silent—sometimes deadly—war of ideologies.

And on the surface everything was unity, a people joined unanimously in their opposition to Castro and his regime in Cuba. But beneath the calm exterior, guerrillas schemed and turned on each other more than on the common enemy. They dealt in secrets, drugs and death, each splinter movement striving to become the voice of a people in exile.

Toro knew the war could reach them there, despite the apparent quiet of the neighborhood. His group might have been seen already, cruising past the target house; armed men might be laying traps to destroy them piecemeal.

With his tiny force, the Cuban warrior could not take a chance on being suckered. He could not afford to sacrifice the slim advantage of surprise. If luck was with them, they could be in and out in moments, their mission accomplished.

He sent one of the gunners, Mano, back around the way that they had come, to discreetly watch the front of the target house. Mano was primed—an Ingram submachine gun underneath his jacket—to cut off the retreat of anyone inside once Toro had penetrated from the rear.

The driver, Rafael, was detailed to stay with the car, making sure that no one tampered with it in their absence. They would need wheels in a hurry, without someone crouching in the back seat or a package wired to explode at the flick of an ignition switch.

Toro recognized the signs of budding paranoia and quickly dismissed them. His fears were not delusions; they were facts of life in the warring camp that was present-day Little Havana.

The final gunner, Emiliano, fell in step with Toro as the leader made his way across a manicured lawn, then down a narrow alley, between the rows of dwellings.

They counted houses, walking along the backside of the residential street they had just traveled, pausing finally before a wooden gate set in a backyard fence. Toro stood on tiptoe to peer over, whistling softly for a dog and getting no response. He finally reached across the gate, feeling for the latch and releasing it, proceeding on inside, his gun probing the way ahead.

Emiliano followed him across the grassy postage-stamp yard, closing rapidly on the back of the house with its covered patio. They brushed past a portable barbecue, and Toro's backup veered away, his pistol drawn now. He paused long enough to check the open door that granted access to a one-car garage connected to the house. When he was satisfied that no one lurked inside, Emiliano nodded, falling into step again at Toro's heel.

They crossed the patio, circling around to the side of the house and up three concrete steps to reach the kitchen door. Standing back against the wall, Toro reached out a hand to test the knob—and found it locked.

He decided there was no way around a violent entry. They had wasted enough time already. Any more delay could spell their deaths.

A glance and nod to Emiliano, and Toro stepped around in front of the kitchen door, his automatic leveled, mentally bracing himself in case bullets started ripping through the flimsy door. He hit the door a flying kick and sent it slamming backward on its hinges, pieces of the cheap pot-metal latching mechanism rattling on the floor inside.

They went in crouching, Toro peeling left, Emiliano right, their weapons cocked and tracking, seeking any sign of hostile life.

The empty kitchen mocked them—but a muffled scuffling from deeper in the house alerted Toro. Moving swiftly through the kitchen down a narrow corridor, he closed on what were obviously bedrooms. Two doors opened off the hallway, one of them ajar, revealing an empty room beyond.

The other door was closed, and in a heartbeat the Cuban identified it as the source of the suspicious sounds.

Toro shouldered the panel, bulled on through into a tiny bedroom. Opposite the door a slender figure was grappling with the window screen, trying to batter it aside and clear a passage.

Toro and Emiliano rushed forward and grabbed him as he threw one leg across the open window's ledge, and finally dragged him back inside the room. The slender man was struggling, kicking out at both of them, a nonstop stream of Spanish curses pouring from his lips. Together they pinned him on the rumpled bed.

Emiliano raised his pistol and whipped it down across the runner's skull. The man went limp. A crimson worm of blood squirmed out from underneath the fallen runner's hairline, crawling down across his face.

The Cuban warrior glanced at his companion and nodded in the direction of the open bedroom doorway.

"La cocina," he snapped, receiving an answering nod from Emiliano.

Each man grabbed an arm of the captive, dragging him off the bed and toward the doorway, through it, back along the dingy corridor.

He was slowly beginning to revive as they reached the small kitchen. Together the Cubans eased him down into a straight-back chair, his head slumped forward, both arms dangling limply at his sides.

Toro produced a pair of handcuffs from a jacket pocket and secured one wrist, then the other, threading the handcuff's chain through a metal rung in back. The shackles kept their prisoner slumped low in his seat, unable to stand or raise his arms.

Emiliano grabbed a handful of his hair and gave the bloodied head a violent shake, gradually bringing the captive around to consciousness. The man was blinking, swallowing hard as a flash of recognition crossed his face. Then his gaze traveled to the gun in Toro's fist.

"Toro," the captive said simply.

"Julio."

Toro recalled the weasel face of Julio Rivera from other days, when they had fought together in the cause of *Cuba libre.* They were allies then, but even so, there had been something out of place about Rivera, something indefinably wrong, which set El Toro's teeth on edge and made him watch the man more closely than he had the other *soldados* in his little clandestine army. When Raoul Ornelas had begun to agitate for mutiny within the ranks, Rivera had been an early convert.

"I want Raoul," Toro told him simply.

"Raoul?"

The man was stalling, trying to come up with something he could use to bargain for his life.

"Si, pendejo. ¿Dónde está? Diga me, pronto."

Rivera managed to dredge up a twisted grimace of defiance, jaw thrust out, lips curling in a sneer.

"*Chinga tu—*"

Emiliano slapped him hard across the back of the skull with his open hand, cutting off the obscene retort, snapping Julio's teeth together sharply.

"*Una vez más* . . . Raoul," Toro repeated patiently.

Rivera glanced warily around at Emiliano, shaking his head as if to clear the ringing in his ears.

"*No sé.*"

Toro shrugged, placing his automatic on the counter beside the sink. He began rummaging through drawers, selecting kitchen implements, examining each in turn before lining them up on the counter top.

A butcher knife.

An ice pick.

A skewer.

A meat cleaver.

Rivera's eyes were widening, and his mouth fell open as he watched Toro walk in front of him to stand before the kitchen stove. The Cuban turned on one of the front burners, a blue gas flame hissing into life inches from his hand.

He brought the butcher knife back over to the stove and propped its blade across the burner, the wide tip distorting the flame. Within moments its razor edge was glowing red, catching a fire of its own and reflecting it into the Cuban's eyes.

Toro turned, leaning back against the counter with his arms crossed, the hissing burner close beside his hip.

"Now, Julio . . . Raoul."

Julio did not respond. Instead he whimpered, struggling with the handcuffs, straining at them until the steel bracelets had worn a bloody groove in both wrists.

"*Bien,* Rivera." Toro's smile was totally devoid of any human feeling.

And Julio Rivera talked.

About Raoul Ornelas. . . Jose 99. . . a great deal more.

When they were finished, forty minutes later, Toro knew he had to get in touch with Bolan. Soon.

The warrior's life—and all their lives—could well be riding on the outcome of that call.

12

Mack Bolan pushed his Firebird eastward, the satchel full of cash on the seat beside him as he left the Club Uhuru, rolling through the heart of Liberty City toward his next target destination. The numbers were falling now, with half a dozen stops to make and no time left to waste.

Liberty City was Miami's ghetto, tucked away just south of the Opa-locka airport, out of sight for most of white Miami, and largely out of mind. On many city maps it was a blank space, the streets ignored as most of the neighborhood's population had also been ignored until very recently.

Black rage had torn the neighborhood apart in recent months, and the scars of that explosion were still visible. The fuse was still sputtering, and every public official in Miami knew that it was only a matter of time until more violence rocked the area. Suspicion, hatred and paranoia on both sides had made the area a pressure cooker, and the lid was ready to blow if someone turned the heat up, even fractionally.

Bolan's target was a numbers countinghouse some six blocks over from the Club Uhuru. The Executioner knew that all the front men and the players would be black, but it was still a Mafia franchise, run behind the scenes by one Dukey Aiuppa.

Aiuppa's real name was Vincenzo, but he won his street name from a string of welterweight bouts he fought professionally before discovering that punching men—or women and children—outside the ring brought higher pay.

Instead of knockouts now, he had a sheet of thirty-five arrests behind him, without a single conviction. A Brooklyn transplant who had worked his way up through the local ranks, Aiuppa ruled his ghetto fiefdom like a colonial warlord, surrounded by stormtroops of all nationalities and colors, reaping sky-high profits from a people mired in poverty and filth.

Aiuppa's countinghouse was tucked away above a pool hall frequented by pimps and pushers. Bolan found his target and parked the Firebird a half block down, unable to get closer because of the Cadillacs and Lincolns lined against the curb on either side of the street. He walked back, feeling hostile eyes upon him as pedestrians turned to stare at his expensive tan-colored suit, dark-brown silk shirt and white silk tie. He drew grim comfort from the Beretta 93-R, which he wore beneath his left arm in a shoulder harness.

He reached the pool hall, pushed on through the swinging doors in front. The pool hall proper was in semidarkness, but he was still able to pick out the scattering of players grouped around two tables on his left. They were watching him, whispering among themselves, but Bolan ignored them, moving between the other deserted tables and on to a flight of wooden stairs set against the back wall of the long, narrow room.

A black man stood on guard at the base of the stairs, watching Bolan approach. He stood with arms crossed,

26.50
6.50
2.25
11.00

back against the banister, prepared to block the Executioner's progress.

"What's happenin'?"

"I'm looking for the Duke," Bolan told him.

"He ain't expectin' any visitors."

Bolan flashed a stony grin.

"Well, let's surprise him."

"He don't like surprises, man."

The Executioner shrugged, the smile softening.

"In that case—"

He moved as if to push on up the stairs past the strong-arm, then pivoted with lightning speed as the guy tried to block him. Bolan ducked beneath a looping right cross, driving the rigid fingers of one hand deep beneath the black man's rib cage, punching the wind out of him and doubling him over.

The Executioner seized an arm and twisted it behind the slugger's back, high up between his shoulders. Then Bolan put his full weight behind the movement as he drove the man into the wall beside the stairs. One hard knee rocketed in, found a kidney once, twice, and the muscle slid to the floor in a boneless sprawl, leaving a blood smear along the wall where his face had made bruising contact with the plaster.

Bolan mounted the stairs, three at a time, barging on through an unguarded door at the top of the landing.

Five startled faces turned to face him, only two of them black. The men were ringed around a small desk piled with money—both bills and coins—and several thousand crumpled betting slips. Bolan quickly recognized the Duke of Liberty City by his broken nose and cauliflower ear.

The soldier nearest to the door was in his shirt-sleeves, wearing iron exposed beneath his arm. He was already moving out to intercept Bolan, but the Executioner brushed past him, not giving any one of them a chance to think coherently.

"Hey, what's this crap?" he demanded, managing to sound outraged as he gesticulated toward the betting slips and cash. "You were supposed to have it packed and ready."

Aiuppa glanced at the closest of his aides, scowling as his eyes returned to Bolan.

"Pack what? Where's Jackson? Who the hell *are* you?"

Bolan knew that Jackson would be sleeping off their brief encounter at the bottom of the stairs.

"You didn't get the word?"

"What word?"

Bolan glared at the Duke. He sounded both suspicious and confused, but he was talking now instead of shooting, and that meant Bolan had a chance to pull it off.

A slim one, yeah—but still a chance.

"The Feds have got a raid lined up," Bolan snapped, checking his watch for emphasis. "With any luck, you may have twenty minutes."

Aiuppa raised a hand, as if asking permission to leave a classroom.

"Hang on there, slick. You can't just waltz in here and—"

"You wanna dick around and flush this bankroll down the crapper?" Bolan asked him furiously. "You think you can afford it, Dukey?"

Aiuppa bristled.

"I guess you'd better tell me just exactly who the hell you are, guy."

Bolan reached into his suit coat, seeing all of them tense, hands edging toward their holstered weapons. He brought out the black ace and skimmed it across the desk at Aiuppa. It landed on a pile of twenties and fifties, directly in front of the welterweight.

Aiuppa stared down at it for a moment as if trying to make sense of what he saw. Looking at Bolan now, Aiuppa seemed hesitant, a touch of fear behind the burning eyes.

"It's been awhile since I saw one of these," he said at last, his voice a bit subdued.

"They're back in style."

Aiuppa's right hand slipped down out of sight, below the lip of the desk top, and Bolan was braced for him to make a move—but now the hand was coming up, still empty, resting palm down on the desk among the bills and coins.

"I'm gonna need authority for this," the mobster said.

"You're looking at it."

Aiuppa straightened up, his shoulders flexing.

"It ain't enough," he said flatly.

Bolan tried to put a touch of sympathy into his mocking smile.

"Okay. You wanna tell the man you pissed away—what is it there, a quarter mil?"

Aiuppa hesitated again, but found the guts to call Bolan's supreme bluff.

"I'll have to take the chance."

Bolan spread his hands in a helpless gesture.

"You called it, Duke," he said. "You live with it—if you can."

Bolan was turning to leave the crowded little office, one hand already sliding toward the open flap of his jacket, when the office door banged open and the black sentry reeled into the room.

There was a pistol in his hand, and he was spluttering with rage, mumbling through battered lips in confusion.

Bolan did not let him have the time to polish up his speech. He chopped down on the man's gun hand with his own hard right, seizing the hood's arm simultaneously and whipping him around. The human projectile hurtled across the room, impacting on the desk and scattering men, money and betting slips in all directions.

The battered gunner ended up atop the desk, his bloody face almost in Duke Aiuppa's lap, driving the Mafia *capo* backward, hard against the wall.

All of them were trying to recover from the explosive interruption as Bolan ripped the 98-R out of side leather, sweeping right to left across the room. In the heat of the moment he knew there was no time for anything fancy now. It was kill or be killed.

The bodycock in shirt-sleeves had his .38 revolver clear and rising, the guy beside him still struggling with an undercover rig. Bolan took them both out with a rapid double punch, 9mm manglers drilling skull, spraying blood and brains across the wall behind them in a gruesome abstract mural pattern.

The Executioner caught another gunner breaking for the sidelines, clawing at a .45 tucked in his belt. Bolan drilled him through the chest with a parabellum round that left him thrashing on the floor.

The man called Jackson was struggling up, rolling off the desk and onto hands and knees beside it, shaking his head like a wounded animal. Bolan's next round took off half of Jackson's face.

Behind the desk Aiuppa was clawing for iron beneath his jacket. The weapon was halfway drawn when a third unseeing eye appeared in the middle of his forehead and the Duke of Liberty City stumbled backward, blood pumping from the ragged hole.

The final gun slick had his weapon out and got a single shot off, gouging plaster over Bolan's head before the Executioner pinned him against a filing cabinet with a deadly 9mm slug.

Bolan moved swiftly to retrieve the black-ace death card, leaving in its place a marksman's medal among the bills and coins.

As he retreated from that kill zone he knew the numbers had run out and the only thing that he could hope for was an easy exit from the pool hall.

He reached the bottom of the stairs and found the poolhall empty. He swiftly crossed the narrow room, striding toward the front doors when he caught a glimpse of movement in the street outside. He hesitated for only a heartbeat as he spotted half a dozen troops leaving a bar across the street. They were all coming his way, two in front unlimbering sawed-off pump shotguns, the others dragging handguns out of hidden leather.

It clicked, suddenly, and Bolan cursed himself for not figuring exactly what was happening when Aiuppa had reached beneath the desk top. The man had pressed a panic button, wired to ring alarms in a nearby building, where Aiuppa's guns would be waiting on the off chance of a call.

Bolan braced his Beretta in both hands, sighting

quickly through a plate-glass window on the lead man, one of the shotgunners. The Executioner fired the instant he made target acquisition. The parabellum drilled a neat hole in the glass, a not so neat one in the gunner's chest, and he went down, his shotgun firing aimlessly into the gutter.

Five guns erupted instantly outside, pumping wild, reflexive rounds into the pool hall, raking windows, walls and furnishings without a clear idea of who or where their human target was. Buckshot and revolver rounds were chewing up the tables, bar, the posters hanging on the dingy, unwashed walls.

To stand and fight was suicide, and Bolan, canny warrior that he was, had other plans.

He doubled back along the length of the room, running in a combat crouch. He held his fire, knowing he would need every round in the Beretta if his plan fell through, if they caught up with him in there or when he made it to the outside.

Bolan found the back door locked from the inside and he kicked his way through it and into the alleyway beyond. Turning right, he could see daylight half a block away. He broke for it, pounding along the alley, Beretta in his fist and ready to answer any challenge at a heartbeat's notice.

He heard the voices, scuffling footsteps on the gravel of the alley at his back, and knew that he would never reach the Firebird, waiting for him at the curb. They were already after him, the first wild rounds impacting on garbage cans and raising clouds of brick dust as they ricocheted off walls to either side.

A shotgun roared, and Bolan ducked instinctively behind a dumpster, nearly deafened as the trash container took the buckshot charge, reverberating like a huge bass drum next to his ear.

Another twenty feet across the no-man's land whistling with blistering rounds, and he would reach the street. There was a chance, a slim one, right, that they would hesitate to follow him out there into the daylight.

Knowing the overwhelming odds, Bolan felt he had no chance but to try. He broke from cover, sprinting for the alley's mouth, ready to receive the searing fusillade that would lift him off his feet and send him spinning into final darkness.

But his move apparently surprised the gunners. They were caught flat-footed, thinking he would stay behind the dumpster long enough for them to throw a tight perimeter around him. Now they began firing wildly.

Bolan reached the mouth of the alley, knowing that the sunlight made his silhouette a perfect target. He was weaving to the right and seeking cover when a fiery red convertible screeched up in front of him, almost knocking him back against the bricks.

A woman was sitting at the wheel, a stunning beauty—and it took no more than a second for the warrior to identify her as the one he had first seen in Tommy Drake's embrace.

She was dressed now, right, but still a dazzler. When she looked at him, the Executioner half expected her to open fire on him with hardware of her own.

Instead, she motioned to him and urgently called out in an excited voice.

"Get in! Please hurry!"

The big warrior quickly figured the odds. He might be leaping out of one fire square into another, but he had no options at the moment. And if Bolan had to take his

chances with an enemy that afternoon, he would prefer
a single woman to an armed platoon of Mafia hardmen
anytime.

She floored the gas and dropped the sportster into
first, screeching out of there with rear tires smoking.
Long before the troop of pistoleros reached the intersection, Bolan and the woman were turning north onto a
major side street, the engine's whine a fading jeer at the
frustrated gunmen.

Riding in the bucket seat beside her, Bolan let himself
relax a notch. But he kept a firm grip on the hot Beretta,
pointing it at the floorboard between his knees. He
might have use of it again at any instant, and the Executioner was not taking anything on faith these days.

A death mask could be beautiful, damn right, and if
he walked into a trap on this one, Bolan would be going
with eyes wide open, primed to kill.

13

"You won't need that with me," the woman told him lightly, glancing down at the Beretta clutched in Bolan's fist.

The warrior hesitated for a moment, then slowly holstered the 93-R.

"I'll keep it all the same," he answered. "Where are we going?"

"Somewhere safe."

"There's no such place."

"Perhaps. But I could not allow you to be killed back there."

The Executioner risked a cautious smile.

"I'm not complaining, just surprised," he said. "You don't hold any grudge for Tommy Drake?"

The young woman made a disgusted sound deep in her throat, and spat out the open window of the drop-top sportster.

"Drake was a pig!"

Mack Bolan raised an eyebrow, curious and surprised by her reaction.

"If you say so."

She read the unspoken question in the soldier's tone, but she was slow in answering. They were rolling along Northwest 103rd Street, heading toward the suburb of Miami Shores. Behind them, the Liberty City ghetto was an ugly fading memory.

They drove along another block or two before the young woman found her voice again.

"I do what must be done," she said, "like you, Matador."

Bolan felt the warning tingle at the base of his skull.

"Have we been introduced?" he asked her, trying to sound casual.

She flashed him a small secret smile.

"There is no need. You're as my sister said."

Bolan frowned, studying her face. And something did a slow rollover in the back of his mind, stirring sluggishly at first, all hazy from the passing years. There was something in her face, around the eyes....

"Your sister?"

"Margarita."

There was age-old sadness in the woman's voice, and the single word hit Bolan like a hard fist underneath the heart. He was silent for an endless moment, first watching her, then turning to regard the passing storefronts, staring through them without seeing anything.

In his mind he pictured Margarita, brave *soldada* of the exile cause. He saw her as she was when last he held her—lifeless, brutalized by mobsters who had tortured her in vain, attempting to find out Bolan's whereabouts. He had found her, found them all in time, and the hot flame of his vengeance had touched off the Miami massacre that followed.

Margarita.

Heaven keep her.

"She was a brave *soldada,*" Bolan said, and knew that even as he spoke the words they sounded lame, inadequate.

A measure of the woman's sadness was replaced by pride as she responded.

"*Sí.* I fight a different war against the animals who killed her needlessly."

"You're undercover?"

She nodded.

"I was placed with Tommy Drake to gather information. He would have been indicted soon."

"I couldn't wait," the warrior said.

"No matter. He did not deserve to live, and it was worth it to be present at his death."

She spoke with an intensity that would have been disturbing had Bolan not understood its source and motivation. He could read the grim commitment in her tone. Everything about her bespoke determination, singleness of purpose.

Some *soldada* in her own right, yeah.

The warrior cleared his throat and changed the subject.

"As long as you're intent on saving me, I ought to know your name."

She smiled at him, a lovely young-old smile.

"Evangelina."

Bolan answered with a small grin of his own.

"What now, Evangelina? You were seen back there—at least your car was seen—and now your cover's blown."

She shrugged.

"It's nothing. This is rented in a different name. I will check in with my control for relocation when we're finished."

"We?"

"I can help you," she told him, plainly reading the sudden distance in his voice.

Bolan shook his head, a firm emphatic negative.

"You've helped enough already. Thanks, but no thanks."

She hung in there, stubborn...like another Cuban tigress he had known. Her eyes flashed at him.

"You think I cannot fight because I am a woman."

"Not at all." He had a sudden flash of Margarita's face, contorted in an endless, soundless scream. "I think you've paid enough dues in a fight that isn't yours."

"It *is* my fight. You think I am afraid of what they did to Margarita? No. I do this thing *because* of her."

"That was another time, Evangelina, and another war. The enemies are different now. The stakes are higher."

"These stakes...can they be higher than a life?" she asked him. "Higher than dignity?"

The Executioner reflected on that briefly, knowing what the lady meant, exactly how she felt...and wanting desperately to keep her out of it.

"You sound a lot like Margarita," he said at last.

"Then you know that I do not give up so easily."

"Okay."

She hesitated, doubting the evidence of her own ears.

"You'll let me help?"

"First things first," he answered. "I lost my wheels back there. I've got a stop to make."

"Just tell me where you need to go. I'll take you there."

"Uh-huh."

He rattled off John Hannon's home address and she repeated it, committing it to memory. They drove awhile in silence, each one occupied with private thoughts, and Bolan felt a certain sense of guilt, a sadness, even, at the double cross he had in mind.

But he could live with guilt, with anger, sadness.

But he did not know if he could live with this one's blood upon his hands, his soul.

He had already cost her far too much. His war had robbed this woman of her family when she was a child. His fight had stripped her of her adolescence and propelled her headlong into danger, into actions that had chipped away her dignity and self-respect.

Mack Bolan did not think less of her because she used her body in pursuit of evidence to put the cannibals away. In fact, he admired her courage and determination. Any guilt was his, he knew, for costing this young one a life of her own, outside the combat zone. She could have been a new bride, settling down somewhere to start a family with a man who loved her. Instead, because of Bolan, she was driving through the streets of Miami with a fugitive, sporting a Mafia price on her head.

The soldier cursed his endless war for robbing this one of her past, and very possibly her future. There was nothing but the present left to reckon with, and he was damned if he would lead her out of danger into greater danger.

Evangelina's sister—brave *soldada*—had paid off the family's dues for generations yet unborn, and there would be no more down payments made to that account if Bolan had a thing to say about it.

If it took a double cross to put this woman-child in safe surroundings, he could live with it, damn right. His war was closing in, the falling numbers gathering momentum, but he would have to make the time to see her out of peril.

To a safe place, yeah.

Except there's no such place.

So, build one. Carve it out of living flesh and blood. The flesh and blood of cannibals and savages.

More than a destroyer, Bolan was a builder, piling clean new stones upon the ruins of the old, erecting something in the nature of a fortress to repel the next attack. Within the walls, at least, there could be safety and security. Outside....

He closed his eyes and let the rhythm of the sports car carry him away.

Outside, there would be Bolan.

14

John Hannon's house was modest, planted in the middle of a quiet residential street in a suburb north of Miami. Bolan had called ahead from a pay phone, and the former captain of detectives was expecting them. As Evangelina swung her convertible into the driveway, Bolan spotted Hannon waiting for them underneath a carport connected to the house.

Hannon greeted them affably, showing mild surprise at his first sight of Bolan's traveling companion. The ex-cop led them through a side entrance into a little family room where he motioned for them to be seated. As he pulled up a chair, Mack Bolan noted a short riot shotgun propped up in a corner, and he realized that Hannon was ready for trouble.

And he wondered if Hannon was ready enough.

"You've been a busy guy," the ex-detective said, settling into a lounger within arm's reach of the pump gun.

"I'm not half done," Bolan answered. "You hearing rumbles?"

Hannon snorted.

"Make that shock waves. They're breaking in on soap operas with news flashes, for heaven's sake. Film at eleven—the whole nine yards."

Bolan chuckled.

"Glad to hear it. I want the word to get around."

"It's getting there," the former cop assured him. "Did you come up with anything?"

Bolan hesitated, glancing at Evangelina. After a moment she got the message, excusing herself, getting directions from John Hannon to the bathroom. The detective watched her go, and Bolan saw him following the sway of her hips with his eyes, studying her appreciatively.

"Where'd you pick her up?"

"Outside Aiuppa's." Bolan saw Hannon's eyebrows raising. "And it was the other way around."

"What's her angle?" Hannon asked.

Bolan put it in a nutshell for him, anxious to make the best use of their dwindling time.

"Federal, undercover. She was working Tommy Drake."

"I'd say she's out of work." Hannon changed gears, shifting topics. "What have you got?"

"I'm working on your Cuban," Bolan told him. "Nothing solid yet, but I'm in touch with someone who may have a handle on him."

Hannon frowned, the deep lines etched into his weathered face.

"Your someone wouldn't be a guy named Toro, would he?"

Bolan met the ex-detective's eyes directly, never flinching.

"You never know."

"It's funny," Hannon said reflectively. "Someone yanked him off the county farm this morning. Got away clean. They're beating every bush from here to Tallahassee."

Bolan remained silent, watching Hannon and waiting

for him to continue. When he spoke again, the former captain of detectives' voice was slow, low pitched.

"I met him once, you know, when I was working Homicide. I had to ask him all about a wild-ass soldier who was shaking up the wise guys."

"Was he helpful?" Bolan asked.

"Like a stone. He told me everything I had to know, and never said a frigging word."

"The Cubans put a premium on loyalty."

"Some others, too, I guess."

Bolan spread his hands.

"There's no way for an Anglo to be inconspicuous among the exiles. If Toro can help me get where I need to go, I'll thank him for the ride."

Hannon's eyes flashed at him.

Bolan frowned. "What did your contacts have to say."

It took a while for Hannon to respond.

Bolan kept studying the man's face. Clearly, he was put off by the thought of breaking convicts out of prison. The guy had worked a lifetime trying hard to put them there and keep them there. It was entirely understandable, but it had no effect on Bolan's combat situation.

Hannon finally made a sour face before he answered Bolan's question.

"A lousy zero. Too damn many street names in the files for them to trace a Jose 99. I couldn't push too hard without inviting interference."

"Never mind. It was a long shot, anyhow." Mack Bolan hesitated, reluctant to involve Hannon any deeper, yet unable to see any way around it. "I need a favor," the Executioner said at last.

"Shoot."

But there was caution in the tone, and Bolan knew that he was skating very near the edge of Hannon's trust, his patience.

Before he had a chance to answer, Evangelina returned from her visit to the washroom. Now her shoulder-length hair was neatly brushed back from her face, and Bolan was again struck by her resemblance to Margarita. He marveled that he had not seen it in her when they met the first time, despite the circumstances...and just as quickly, he wondered how much of it might be simply the product of his own imagination.

Either way, the lady was a living monument to something from the past, another stop along the hellfire trail of Bolan's private, endless war. A part of Margarita lived in her, through her, and he would do everything within his power to preserve that vestige, let it blossom and grow into everything that it could be.

"Where are we going next?" she asked, addressing herself to both men at once, but focusing her main attention on the Executioner.

He looked her square in the eye before he answered.

"Not we, Evangelina. You'll be staying here awhile... for safety's sake."

He registered the startled glance from Hannon, but there was no time to ask the favor now. Bolan focused on the lady now, reading anger and betrayal in her face.

"Staying?" she asked incredulously. "No! I saved your life. I brought you here."

The soldier nodded.

"And I appreciate it. That's one reason why I can't risk taking you along."

There was a flicker of surprise beneath the brooding anger.

"One reason? What is the other?"

"I move better on my own. You'd slow me down, get one or both of us killed."

The lady looked a little hurt at first, but she recovered swiftly, temper and a flaring irritation taking over from the wounded pride.

"I can protect myself, *señor*. I am a warrior, *una soldada*—like you."

"Oh, no, you're not." Bolan rose from his chair, advancing on her, pleased that she did not flinch away from him. "You're not like me at all, Evangelina. When was the last time you killed a man? Can you remember how the blood smelled? How his brains looked when you held the gun against his head and dropped the hammer?"

As he spoke the soldier aimed an index finger at her pretty face, the fingertip coming to rest between her eyes.

She shivered at his touch but did not pull away.

Bolan bored in, unrelenting, hating the hurt he had put in her eyes, knowing there was no soft way around the obstacle.

"You ever slit a throat, Evangelina? Do you know the way it feels to saw through flesh and gristle like you're carving a roast, except the roast's still fighting for its life?"

A single tear made a glistening track across one cheek.

"I've never killed a man," she said, the voice soft, shaking. "But I could. I know it."

"Don't be eager," Bolan told her, letting softness creep into his voice now.

He cupped her face gently in his palm, tenderly wiping away the tear.

"I am a soldier," she repeated.

"Fine. So live to fight another day."

She was resisting, but more weakly now.

"I choose my fights," she said softly, tearfully.

And Bolan knew he had her now.

"Sorry. This one's taken."

"And if I refuse to stay behind?"

It was a question more than a challenge. He could sense that most of the fight had drained out of her now.

"I don't have time to argue with you now," he said. "You know what I say is true." He paused, letting that sink in, waiting until she nodded, a barely perceptible motion of her head. "I'll need your car keys."

Another moment's hesitation, then she fished around inside her purse, finally coming out with them and handing them over to Bolan. He turned toward Hannon, frowning, knowing he had put the former captain of detectives on the spot.

"I'll be back when I can," he said.

If I can.

And Bolan pushed the grim, defeatist thought away from him as he shook hands with Hannon at the door. Behind the ex-cop, he could see Evangelina watching him, but she did not respond when Bolan waved his hand in parting.

"We'll be here," Hannon told him, glancing briefly at the lady.

Evangelina nodded, finally.

"Sí."

And Bolan put that house behind him, hoping those two good people would be safe along the sidelines of his war. There were no guarantees, he knew, but at the same time he had done his utmost, short of backing off completely while he saw the lady to some haven out of town or out of state.

There was no time for backing off or backing down, the warrior knew from grim experience. The battle had been joined there in Miami, and although he still had no firm handle on the situation, he knew that there was only one direction he could travel on the hellfire trail.

His course was dead ahead and damn the enemy's defenses. The Executioner had come to shake Miami, and nothing short of death would stop him from accomplishing that aim.

He was rattling Miami, see what fell out of the vipers' nest.

And he would see Evangelina when he got the chance.

If he got the chance.

In the meantime, there were cannibals at large, demanding Bolan's full attention. He was carrying the fire. And someone in Miami was about to feel the heat.

15

Raoul Ornelas listened to the ringing of the telephone on the other end, his anger and frustration mounting by the moment.

Seven.

Eight.

Nine.

On the tenth ring he slammed down the receiver, cursing under his breath. It was a gesture out of place with the man's normal sense of control, but he could feel the cool slipping, giving way to the bottled emotions that he felt inside.

He had been trying to reach Julio Rivera, his second-in-command, all morning, ever since the news reports had started coming in, and so far there had been no answer.

Frustration gave way to puzzlement and Ornelas frowned. It was not like Julio to be away from home throughout the morning hours; even when he spent the evening with a woman, Julio never slept over, preferring the security of home.

Healthy paranoia kept his second-in-command alive. And that same paranoia, multiplied by the tempo of current events, told Ornelas again that something must be wrong.

Beneath his anger now there was something else—an

uneasiness that bordered on fear. It was uncustomary for the Cuban to feel anything but self-assurance, but on the other hand, he had a lot to worry about these days.

Too many strange and unexpected things were going on around Miami for a man to feel secure. Within the past twelve hours ominous bits and pieces of a grim mosaic had been casually revealed to him, and now he felt the very fabric of his world beginning to unravel around him.

Ornelas stopped himself, cutting off the train of thought before it could progress to its logical conclusion. The *soldado* knew that he would need his wits about him if he was to cope with the several riddles that the past half day had handed to him.

And a quick solution to those riddles might be vital. To completion of the plan he had been nurturing along for months...to his very survival, if it came down to that.

He needed answers in a hurry—but the worst part of it was that, so far, he was still uncertain of the questions.

First things first. There was the death—no, the *assassination* of Tommy Drake the previous night. Someone had entered Drake's *estancia* and murdered him, along with several of his hardmen, making off again without disturbing anything around the place, from all reports. No robbery, no vandalism—nothing.

That made it an assassination, by professionals. It also cut off Ornelas's supply of cocaine for the moment and placed him in the uncomfortable position of having to seek out new contacts. He could handle it, but it was just another inconvenience, something else to occupy his mind at the very moment when concentration was so vital.

He wondered if the hit on Drake could be related to the near miss on John Hannon. Somehow, Drake's best men had failed to take the nosy private eye, and they had gotten themselves killed in the bargain. Ornelas had no faith in mere coincidence. He realized that the events were probably related, but beyond that realization he could not proceed. Without some leads, at least a clue to the identity of Drake's assassins. . . .

No matter how it read, the failure to eliminate Hannon left some dangerous loose ends. He would have to try and snip them off before they had a chance to multiply like roaches in the woodwork.

Toro's jailbreak, naturally, had been the worst news of the day—hell, of the year. The timing, on the eve of Ornelas's bold scheme, could not be automatically dismissed as chance. If there was some dark, guiding hand behind it. . . .

Briefly he reflected on the string of violent incidents around Miami through the morning hours and early afternoon, all seemingly directed at the operations Drake and Phillip Sacco had their fingers in: drugs, gambling, women.

Raoul Ornelas had not survived so long on the fringes of the underground by trusting chance or letting others do his thinking for him. He was worried now, and with good reason. Something was afoot around Miami and right now he did not have a clue as to what might be going on.

Ignorance was no way to survive in war. And it was war that had taught him to survive. He stared at the phone as he recalled the past.

As a teenager he had fought for Castro against the animal Batista, battling to release his native Cuba from a tyranny that had oppressed her people for a generation. He had lost a brother in the fight and counted it a small price to be part of history.

He had survived to see the people's revolution twisted and transformed into something else, with the appearance of the Soviet "advisors" and Fidel's admission that he was, indeed, a secret Communist.

When exiles started fleeing from their homeland to the coast of Florida, Ornelas went with them, vowing that someday he would return and finish what he had started as a young guerrilla in the mountains.

He had joined the anti-Castro movement in Miami at a time when it was smiled on by the U.S. government. He felt betrayed by the movement he had risked his life for, and he sought a way to win revenge against his traitors. The CIA had helped him hone his martial skills, and at the same time they had taught him all the grim realities of power politics, of working with the Mafia to gain your end results, of using anyone and anything that might aid the cause.

Then tragedy struck the Ornelas family again. Raoul had lost another brother at the Bay of Pigs, cut down by Castro's gunners on the beach when American air support failed to arrive on schedule. He had seen the exile movement betrayed by so-called friends, the U.S. pulling back support and closing down the training camps in Florida and Louisiana, harassing the movement's leaders, opening relations, finally, with Fidel.

To Raoul Ornelas, the missile crisis, all the rest of it since 1961, was window dressing. He was learning quickly that the end result was all that mattered. Never mind the changing cloak of ideology that could be donned and then discarded in an instant, for convenience.

Power and wealth were the keys, and he was determined to secure them at any cost.

Ornelas served himself now, working free-lance for anyone who paid his price. Today, the price was brought by drugs and terrorism in the proper cause.

But it was tomorrow that worried him. A violent storm was clearly brewing in Miami and he could not tell which direction the wind was coming from. And now, somehow, Toro was on the loose again, perhaps already looking for him.

They had been friends once, Ornelas and Toro, back when both of them were young, idealistic *soldados* in the cause of *Cuba libre*. Somehow, Toro never quite outgrew naive idealism. He still believed in capital-*J* justice for the people. He resisted all attempts to see the light. That made him an obstruction; one that had to be removed in order for Raoul Ornelas to advance himself.

Removal had been surprisingly easy. Toro's trust, his sense of honor and loyalty, worked against him in the end. He refused to see that there were those around him who would betray him if the price was right.

Ornelas had balked at killing Toro. It was a tactical mistake that Ornelas now believed he would soon regret. At the time it had seemed enough to frame Toro, pack him off to prison. By the time he won release, Ornelas would have Toro's soldiers safely locked into Raoul's own private army. They would be seeing more action, making more money. And when—if—Toro won parole, he would be a forgotten man.

Except he was out right now, and suddenly, things were starting to go sour for Raoul Ornelas.

He felt himself becoming more and more agitated by the moment, trying desperately to keep control of his emotions, of his men. His very life, he knew, depended on his ability to lead, to fill his men with confidence and make them do his bidding gladly.

So far, everything had gone according to Ornelas's master plan, the pieces falling into place as if by destiny. At the final hour, everything was ready. The money—most of it, at any rate—had already been deposited in Ornelas's clandestine bank account.

The thought of his employer only made Ornelas worry more. He had accepted payment, promised to perform...and now, he was beginning to have deadly second thoughts. Too late to call the operation off, of course; there would be no way to stop it. But for the first time in a long career of fighting for assorted causes, Ornelas had doubts about his own ability to pull a mission off.

And why had Toro's break come *now,* with Ornelas's biggest operation yet less than a day away? Toro might spoil everything—by bringing down the heat from his escape on Little Havana, or by himself, in his quest for revenge.

Ornelas knew that Toro blamed Raoul for Toro's time in jail. It had not taken the canny exile leader long to decide exactly who had fingered him. While he was in the lockup, Toro's rage was impotent, wasted on the walls that held him captive. Now he was free to track Ornelas, to take whatever action his enraged mind could conceive of.

Ornelas wondered who had helped his former friend escape. Someone was supporting him, at least with tactical assistance on the break itself—and that was what

concerned Ornelas most of all. Alone, El Toro was a
thorn in his side. But with support troops, a secret army
of his own, he might turn out to be a dagger in the heart.

Ornelas felt his control slip another notch, knew that
he was rapidly losing the battle to keep his wits about
him. He knew what to expect if anything went wrong
with the operation at this late date.

He decided to consult with his control on this one,
brief him on what had been happening around Miami in
the past twelve hours. If the man was dense enough to
somehow miss the daily news, he had some shocks in
store for him. And maybe he would have some ideas of
how Ornelas could keep things from disintegrating into
chaos.

Maybe.

There was a single heartbeat's tremor in his hand as
he reached for the telephone receiver. At the last instant, he hesitated, deciding to try Julio Rivera one last
time before he took the final step.

If he could reach Rivera, they could get together and
work out something on their own without involving
Ornelas's sponsors.

He started dialing slowly. But his mind was racing,
checking out contingencies, alternatives. Beneath it all,
he wondered where a man could hide himself when his
world went up in smoke.

16

The Cuban embassy located in Miami is a minifortress, built to keep its occupants inside and all intruders out. Some ninety miles from home, surrounded by the hostile thousands of their countrymen, the members of the consulate do not take any chance with security.

The gardeners who tend the yard and flower gardens so solicitously are, in fact, armed guards. With darkness, more traditional uniformed sentries take their place, prepared to shoot first and ask questions later.

The ornate wrought-iron gates, watched by uniformed patrols and television cameras, are reinforced to stop—or at least slow down—most vehicles available to rank-and-file civilians.

The ten-foot wall of masonry around the compound is surmounted by a coil of razor wire, protected by electronic sensors. Strategically positioned trees screen the embassy from the view of sightseers—or snipers; its windows are of special bulletproof glass, incorporating wire mesh to deflect rifle grenades and contain the initial blast within a restricted area. Inside the *Fidelista* outpost, no one is ever really quite at ease.

In case of an attack on the embassy, no self-respecting terrorist would bother with Jorge Ybarra's office on the second floor. Ybarra was well-known around Miami as the cultural attaché of the Cuban mission, a man attuned to finer things than politics—such as art, good literature, vintage wine.

But the FBI and CIA agents realized Ybarra was, in fact, Miami station chief for Castro's secret police, the DGI—Dirección General de Inteligencia. It was a covert outfit infamous throughout the western hemisphere for its involvement in exporting Castro's revolution to reluctant customers. In many cases, the organization was little more than an extension of the Soviet KGB; at other times, its officers came up with plans and exercises of their own, inevitably aimed at weakening prestige of the United States, advancing communism in Latin America or the Caribbean.

And agents of the DGI had surfaced everywhere the Cubans had a military presence—in Grenada, once upon a time, in Africa, in Nicaragua.

An early Castroite, Jorge Ybarra chose the service like a careful shopper picking out a suit he knows will fit him for a lifetime. He took to the clandestine world at once, a natural. He fought beside Guevara in Bolivia, before the roof fell in and Che was sold into captivity and death by traitors. As a charter member of the DGI, he had done service for Fidel in Chile, in El Salvador and elsewhere, prior to his posting with the Miami consulate.

Ybarra's specialty was terrorism and insurgency. He had been schooled by masters in Havana, completed training at Patrice Lumumba University inside the Soviet Union. The people's revolution had a use for terrorists now, with victory hanging in the balance for a dozen Third World nations. And Ybarra was the man to see about arranging incidents, assassinations—anything and everything along the lines of raw guerrilla warfare in an urban setting.

As noon approached, the section chief of DGI was alone in his office, mulling over the final details for his greatest coup to date. Everything was in readiness; all had been running smoothly until very recently, and he was beginning to feel some small concern that something might be going wrong.

Jorge Ybarra never worried. He was sometimes puzzled, but never for long; he was occasionally concerned, but only until he could figure out a plan of action to remove the momentary inconvenience. At no time did he seriously consider failure as an option in his plans.

Ybarra was nothing if not effective. In his thinking, problems existed to be solved. They were tests of his native ingenuity and he welcomed them, most of the time.

But he did not welcome any of the things that he was hearing from his contacts on the streets of Miami. His agents in the exile community and in the syndicate were passing on disturbing news.

Another man might have been worried, even discouraged. As it was Ybarra felt concern.

There were some minor storm clouds building up on the horizon, true, but he felt confident that everything would go ahead on schedule.

The private phone on his desk was shrilling and the cultural attaché frowned. He waited through three rings before he reached cautiously for the receiver.

Only a handful of men in the city knew this number, and he was not expecting calls from any of them at the moment. Unexpected news was often bad, and now Ybarra steeled himself for what would almost surely be another problem.

"*¿Sí?*"

"This is Jose."

"I recognize your voice," he told the caller.

"Is this line safe?"

"Of course."

Ybarra had his people check the line each morning, scanning carefully for any sign of taps, any sort of interception that might indicate the FBI was listening in on his private phone. In times of crisis, as of late, he had the lines checked several times each day—and they were clean as of three hours ago.

"There may be trouble," his caller said cryptically.

"Oh?"

Ybarra kept his voice calm, noting a hesitation, a surprise at his reaction in the caller's own shaky tone.

"You've heard the news?"

"I hear much news. Be more specific."

"Toro. Drake. The rest of it."

"What rest?"

He felt concern, but was careful to keep all traces of it from his voice.

"There have been shootings, incidents...."

Ybarra released his breath in a weary sigh.

"There are incidents every day," he said, allowing a trace of annoyance to surface in his tone.

"Not like this. I am afraid—"

"I see."

"I am afraid the plan may be in jeopardy," the caller continued.

"You exaggerate."

"But Toro—"

"One man. Hunted. Outcast. He is nothing."

"And Tommy Drake?"

Another sigh, this time audible over the line.

"These gangsters kill each other regularly. Why concern yourself with their misfortunes?"

"But if there is some connection...."

"*Basta!* That's enough! You are creating problems in your mind where none exist." Having delivered the reprimand, he allowed his tone to soften. "Rest easy. Everything is ready. Every possibility has been accounted for. You told me yourself."

The caller cleared his throat, and when he spoke again he sounded calmer but still uncertain of himself.

"I know, but—"

"No more, now." Ybarra cut him off. "You represent the people's revolution. All the masses put their faith in you. Be worthy of their trust. If nothing else, be worthy of the price you have received."

The caller almost choked on his reply.

"*Sí. Comprendo.*"

"*Bien.*"

Before the other man could think of something else to say, Ybarra cradled the receiver. He was certain that "Jose" had understood his meaning, thinly veiled behind his spoken words. The project's ultimate success or failure rested on his shoulders, and if it should fail, then he would have to bear the burden.

The cultural attaché thought of Tommy Drake and his assassination. It would hamper drug trade in the south of Florida, but only briefly, virtually unnoticeable at street level, where the pushers and consumers made their deals. Another Tommy Drake would come along, perhaps before the day was out, and the flow of pure cocaine and heroin from Cuba would continue as before.

As for the man called Toro, his escape from prison might be cause for some concern—but only to his caller.

Jorge Ybarra had no more to fear from Toro than he did from any of the countless other rightist exiles living in Miami. Any one of them would kill him, but he refused to let them have the chance.

Ybarra was a survivor by instinct and by training. He intended to go on surviving in the cause that he had chosen for his own.

No matter if the several strange events should be connected by some stronger thread than mere coincidence. It was a troubling thought, but Ybarra finally dismissed it as unlikely—or, in any case, too little and too late to sabotage his plans. The wheels were greased, already in motion, and within twenty-four hours they would be grinding over anyone who tried to oppose him.

The stage was set for ultimate humiliation of the Anglo-capitalist pigs, and very soon now, they would taste the kind of terror that was a staple in the Third World diet.

Ybarra smiled and lit a thin cheroot, inhaling the acrid smoke and expelling it toward the ceiling. Another day, less now, and he would see his master plan fulfilled. Nothing, no one, could stand in his way.

If anything went wrong, he would off-load responsibility upon his second-in-command, the worried caller. And if this man Toro was still hunting for the one who called himself Jose, Ybarra just might let them find each other. It would be amusing.

The sudden laughter welled up out of him spontaneously, and filled the office. His secretary, if she heard him, might suspect that he was drinking, but Ybarra did not care.

He was about to score the coup of his career, and there was not an obstacle in sight.

His enemies, the Anglos, were about to learn exactly what it felt like to exist with terror. And Ybarra would enjoy his role as teacher in that lesson.

17

Well back from the picture window of John Hannon's house, out of sight of anyone outside, Evangelina sat watching the street.

Hannon's low-pitched voice rumbled across the room.

"You've known him long?" the ex-detective asked.

It took a heartbeat for the young woman to realize who he was talking about.

"Not long," she said. "We only met last night."

She flashed back briefly to the scene at Tommy Drake's, blushing involuntarily at the image of herself, nude on the bed with the mobster on top of her, the man in black looming over them both, clutching death in his hand. She could still recall the rush of fear, thinking that it was a Mob hit coming down, herself included in the cast of victims. Fear, and then the sweet, almost guilty feeling of relief when it was done and she was spared from death.

"I understand you helped him out this morning," Hannon said, trying to sound casual.

Evangelina shrugged.

"It was a small thing."

Hannon nodded, giving her an understanding smile.

"Sure. With me it was the other way around. A small thing. All he did was save my life."

Evangelina looked at him with new awareness.

"You care about him, don't you?"

Hannon looked embarrassed and confused at the same time.

"Lady, I don't know exactly what I care about these days." His voice softened as he asked her, "You?"

"My sister knew him long ago." She hesitated, trying hard to think of something else to say, some way to finish it. "She . . . died."

A look of understanding passed across the former captain of detectives' face.

"I . . . I had no idea. . . ."

The telephone rang, before either of them could dredge up further conversation.

Hannon left his chair and crossed to the phone, picking it up on the third ring. From her position by the window, Evangelina could watch him and eavesdrop on his side of the conversation.

Hannon was silent for a long moment, listening to the caller. At length, his brow deeply furrowed, he said, "I'm listening."

After another twenty-second pause, he glanced over at Evangelina with a look that might have been concern—or guilt.

"I can find it," he said at last, turning his wrist for a look at his watch. "Yes . . . no problem."

Hannon looked worried as he cradled the receiver. Moving back into the living room he stood beside the window for a long, silent moment, staring out into the quiet street before he spoke again.

"I have to go out for a while," he told her simply. "You should be safe here if you stay inside."

Evangelina shook her head.

"I'm coming with you."

"I told the man I'd keep you safe," he said.

"You said that you would *stay* with me," she countered, reading irritation in the large man's face, refusing to be cowed by it.

Hannon looked flustered, his face reddening.

"I can't afford to take you. There's no way for me to guarantee your safety."

Evangelina let him see a cryptic little smile.

"There's no way you can guarantee another." And then she played her ace. "You leave me here, I follow you. There's nothing you can do to keep me here."

He mulled that over for a moment, finally making up his mind.

"All right. I want your word you'll stick with me and do exactly what I tell you, when I tell you. Agreed?"

"*Sí*. I will."

Hannon disappeared into a narrow hallway leading to the bedrooms. When he reemerged he was wearing a jacket and there was a revolver in his hand. He broke the cylinder and checked the load, then slipped it into a holster that he wore beneath his jacket, on his belt. The eyes that met hers across the room were made of flint.

"You armed?"

Evangelina nodded. She produced a small automatic pistol that she carried in her handbag.

As Hannon showed her out and locked the door behind them, Evangelina's mind was racing on ahead. She wondered if she had the strength and courage that it took to kill a man; if she was equal to the challenge posed to her by the man she knew as El Matador. Perhaps she would lose her nerve, get herself and Hannon killed through cowardice or stupidity.

The young woman stiffened, shaking off the fears. Inside, she knew that she would do whatever might be necessary to avenge her sister, to become a part of Matador's unending battle.

And it finally seemed, in spite of everything, that she might have an active part to play in that crusade. She looked forward to the opportunity—and not without a trace of fear—but she would not permit John Hannon, *anyone,* to rob her of her destiny.

Her sister, Margarita, had died in this cause. Now Evangelina had a chance to live for it, and she was holding on with both hands, refusing to let go while life remained.

THE CHEVY WAS A LOANER. Hannon's car would not be patched up before Monday, and in the meantime he insisted on remaining mobile. Now pushing borrowed wheels south along the Dixie Highway, he was thankful that he had insisted on the car when his was towed off from the shooting scene.

He had not recognized the caller's voice. It had been a different voice from the one that had suckered him the day before, but Hannon knew that the identity of individual callers probably meant next to nothing.

It was the message that had riveted him instantly, compelled him to risk another ambush, violate the trust that had been placed upon his shoulders. He could hear the words inside his mind, as if the caller had been sitting in the back seat, whispering in his ear.

"You looking for some trucks? Some guns? I know where you can find them."

The caller had provided the directions for a meeting, and Hannon, dammit, had agreed to everything.

Of course, the meet could be another trap. He recognized the risk; his memories of his brush with death were vivid in his mind. He knew the possibility—hell, the probability—that he was walking into mortal danger . . . but at least this time he would be going into it with both eyes open, armed and ready.

The woman, now, she was a problem for him. Bolan had surprised him with her, dumping her into his lap that way. And Hannon now had compounded the problem by dragging her along on what could prove to be a lethal wild-goose chase.

The lady was a veteran of sorts, by Bolan's own admission. Hannon would watch out for her as best he could, but in the last analysis it would be every man or woman fighting solo for survival.

The way it had always been, sure.

They were following the Dixie Highway, crossing out of Broward County into Dade, when Hannon picked out the Caddy crew wagon in his rearview mirror. He felt the old familiar chill race up his spine, his palms suddenly moist where they gripped the steering wheel.

The tail was gaining. He could make out hostile faces behind the broad, tinted windshield. Reaching inside his jacket he drew the Colt Python .357 Magnum out of its holster and laid it on the seat beside him.

The woman saw his move and craned around in her seat, following Hannon's gaze, picking up the tail through the window.

And Hannon was surprised at the look of grim determination on her face as she pulled the little nickel-plated autoloader from her handbag, jacking back the slide to chamber up a live one.

Their eyes met briefly, and he found something inside

there that he had seldom seen in the eyes of combat-hardened veterans. Strength, a hard, indomitable will—all tempered by a healthy fear of what was coming.

Some lady, right.

They shared a fleeting smile and then his eyes were on the road, his mind fully occupied with their immediate predicament. He milked some more speed from the Chevy's straining engine, but the more powerful Caddy was chewing up the distance between the two vehicles. The crew wagon's grill was inches from their bumper now, and Hannon flirted with the thought of slamming on his brakes, forcing them into a collision and coming out with all guns blazing while they were still dazed.

Just as quickly he saw the gun muzzles nosing up above the dashboard, recognized the automatic weapons back there and abandoned the idea.

Any chance they had remained in flight now. Standing still, they could only be cut to ribbons by the gun crew.

Suddenly the Caddy surged around them, gaining on the driver's side, pulling abreast. In his side mirror, then through the window itself, Hannon could see weapons jutting from the power windows as they slid down, opening a field of fire.

John Hannon cranked desperately on his own window handle, using all his strength, and he had the glass almost halfway down before the handle came off in his hand with a resounding snap. Cursing wildly, he dropped the useless crank and snared his Python from the seat beside him, lifting it and trying hopelessly to find an angle through the half-open window.

He was tightening into the squeeze when the guns in the Caddy erupted, raking his Chevy with a shattering broadside. Glass flew everywhere, jagged shards embedding themselves in his cheek and throat. Bullets drilled through the door and bodywork, one of them tracing fire across his thighs, another boring deep into his side, reaming vital organs along the way.

Hannon lost control of the Chevy, doubling over the wheel as the car jounced across the shoulder, swerving off pavement onto gravel, finally grass. The Caddy swept on past them, one parting burst turning the windshield into crystals, the glass suddenly imploding in a thousand pebbled pieces.

On the seat beside him he heard Evangelina scream, then the car was plowing shrubbery under, straining at the leafy barrier and finally stalling out amidst the ruins of a demolished hedgerow.

Through a haze of pain John Hannon was aware of everything around him. He could feel the blood puddling in his lap, the throbbing of his wounds, a creeping chill that could only mean one thing.

As if from far away he heard the engine ticking, slowly cooling down, and beneath the hood, a steady dripping from the hoses severed by the broadside fusillade. It might be gasoline, he knew, but suddenly it did not seem to matter.

Something was holding his legs down, and Hannon realized that his gun arm was also pinned against his side. Glancing down, vision blurry from the blood of ragged scalp wounds streaming across his face, he recognized the girl.

She had fallen toward him when the Chevy came to rest. Now her head was resting in his lap, her shoulder jammed against his forearm, pinning it against his seat.

It took only a glance to tell the veteran of Homicide that she was gone. The bullet's entry wound above one eye was tiny, but the fist-sized exit pit behind her ear had taken everything inside and scattered it across the back seat of his loaner.

She was dead as hell, and rising through the pain, John Hannon felt a sudden sense of failure. He had promised Bolan that he would protect the girl, and now he was directly responsible for killing her. He might as well have pulled the frigging trigger personally.

The fingers of his right hand still were locked around the Python's grip, and Hannon tried to free his hand from underneath her. He had to get out of there while wounded legs and leaking veins still had the strength to carry him away.

The girl was out of it, and Hannon had to think in terms of personal survival.

Reaching down, he tried to lift her head, and in the process saw that much of the blood pooling down between his legs was hers.

He was reaching for the door handle, when a hulking shadow loomed beside the car. A man-shape blotted out the sinking sun and cast sudden darkness across the wounded and the dead.

They had, of course, returned to check their score.

He should have seen it coming, known that on the second hit they would not risk another near-miss foul-up.

Hannon tugged at the Magnum. Its front sight snagged in the material of Evangelina's bloodstained blouse, digging into a lifeless breast. He tried to curse, but at the moment he could muster nothing louder than a whimper.

The hitter raised a weapon—Hannon recognized it as

an Uzi—and he racked the cocking lever back to chamber up a round.

"It's checkout time," the hitter told him, grinning.

Hannon closed his eyes and let the darkness carry him
away.

18

Bolan saw the flashing multicolored lights ahead and started braking, letting other traffic pass him by, already looking for a place to park the dark, unmarked sedan. He had exchanged the car for Evangelina's conspicuous sportster an hour earlier, meaning to return her car later, but now he feared that he would never have the chance.

He had been drawn there by a shooting broadcast over the portable police-band monitor he carried in the car. The dispatcher named John Hannon as a victim, fate unknown, and there was mention of an unnamed female in the car.

It was enough.

He drove now with a lead weight sitting in the center of his chest, precisely where his heart should be. He found a place on the grassy shoulder of the highway and scanned the scene up ahead: an ambulance, the back doors standing open; state police cars and other unmarked vehicles belonging to the men from Metro Homicide. The uniforms and plainclothes officers were mingling on the shoulder of the highway, watching as two paramedics carried a sheet-draped figure toward the open rear of the meat wagon. Inside, another body was visible, already strapped to a stretcher and ready to go.

Bolan felt the life drain out of him. His pulse was

pounding in his ears. Across the narrow span of manicured grass a nondescript Chevrolet was buried nose into a hedge, and from where he sat the Executioner could see the shattered windows, the bullet holes that pocked the fading paint job.

A motorcycle cop in helmet, shades and jackboots was approaching him, one hand raised in warning as Bolan alighted from the car, his face carved into a scowl.

"I'm sorry, sir, you'll have to move along. This is official business."

Bolan let him see the fake credentials briefly, snapping the wallet shut and returning it to an inside pocket before the officer could study it in detail.

"LaMancha, Justice," he snapped. "It's as official as they come. Who's in charge here?"

"That's Captain Wilson, sir." The motor officer pointed through the little crowd of shifting bodies. "Over there."

Bolan followed his aim to a man in a gray three-piece suit. He was standing slightly apart from the rest, staring at the bullet-ridden Chevy. The name touched a bell in his memory, calling up fragmented images of another time, another Miami.

Wilson had worked under Hannon in Homicide, if he recalled correctly. And now he was in at the finish.

A finish for which warrior Bolan was at least partly responsible, yes.

Bolan moved toward Wilson, brushing past a pair of uniformed patrolmen. He passed the ambulance, refusing to look inside at the bloody shrouded figures.

At his approach, the captain turned, his reverie interrupted. He greeted the new arrival with a frown.

"Help you?"

Bolan waved the spurious credentials past his face and pocketed them again.

"Frank LaMancha, Justice."

Wilson's frown remained in place; if anything, it deepened.

"Bob Wilson, Metro," he replied. "Something here that interests you?"

"I caught the bulletin about your man."

When Wilson spoke again there was suppressed emotion in his voice.

"Not mine," he said at last. "He was retired."

"But working."

Wilson looked and sounded wary when he answered.

"Strictly private."

"Looks like someone made it public."

Wilson did not respond immediately. He was looking past Bolan now, back at the bullet-punctured car that had taken John Hannon on his last ride.

"I guess."

"You make the girl yet?" Bolan asked.

Wilson shook his head.

"Latino, probably a Cuban. Young. She had a gun, but no ID. We're checking on it."

"Maybe you should try the federal building," Bolan told him.

The homicide detective raised an eyebrow. "Yeah? What was she, an informer?"

"It's not for me to say. I'd ask for SOG."

Wilson's stern face registered an immediate reaction, quickly covered by the frown. It was obvious to Bolan that the captain was familiar with the federal Sensitive Operations Group. Once headed by Hal Brognola, it was still closely supervised by the big Fed from Washington Wonderland, dealing in cases too sensitive for other federal agencies to handle comfortably.

"So," Wilson said, "it's like that, is it?"

Bolan kept it cryptic.

"Could be."

"Is that your interest?"

"Oh, I'm interested in a lot of things—like trucks and guns." He paused, letting that sink in before he dropped the second shoe. "Like Jose 99."

Another reaction from Wilson, this one harder to conceal.

"You know the name?" Bolan prodded.

"I've heard it."

It was obvious to Bolan that the officer was holding something back.

"Know where I can find him?" he asked, probing.

Wilson made a disgusted face.

"If I did, he'd be downtown right now." He hesitated, clearly reluctant to say more, but finally continued, as if against his own better judgment. "The FBI says it has something on him from a routine wiretap on the Cuban embassy. He calls the cultural attaché there from time to time. They haven't traced him yet."

"You tie him in with this?" Bolan asked.

"I wouldn't rule it out," the homicide detective answered. He cast an almost wistful glance in the direction of the ambulance. "It looks like John was really onto something after all."

"He never knew the half of it," the Executioner said.

"And you do?"

"I'm getting there."

But even as he spoke, Bolan knew he was no closer to

solving the puzzle now than when he had first started. So far all he had were scattered, scrambled pieces of the puzzle, and collecting them had proved a very costly process. Someone would have to pay dearly for Bolan to break even.

And he was looking forward now to the collection of that debt.

"You ready to coordinate?" the homicide detective asked him, breaking in on Bolan's train of thought.

"It's premature," he answered.

"I see." Bob Wilson stared at Bolan. "I don't take well to being frozen out, LaMancha. This one cuts too close to home."

Mack Bolan read the emotion in his voice and realized that it was genuine.

"If I were you," he said, "I'd take a look at Tommy Drake."

"You're late," the officer replied. "He's history."

"He had connections," Bolan responded. "Some of them were interested in Hannon's work."

"I know about the Stomper," Wilson said.

"Then you know that he was acting under orders."

Wilson feigned incredulity.

"Really? What was your first clue?"

"No offense, Captain. It never pays to overlook the obvious."

"We won't be overlooking anything," Wilson answered, but his voice and face were softening already.

Bolan shifted gears, taking off along another tack.

"You know a Cuban activist named Raoul Ornelas?"

Wilson raised an eyebrow at the change of pace.

"Everybody knows Ornelas. He's Omega 7. Are you connecting him to this?"

Bolan shrugged again. "Omega 7 needs the hardware. Hannon might have been too close."

Wilson shook his head, a discouraging expression on his face. "You're drifting. First the Mob, then Cuban exiles. What's the angle?"

"Sacco and the exiles go way back together. You know that as well as I do. They could be hand in glove."

"I thought about that, yeah," the officer conceded. "But what does Sacco need with military weapons?"

"It might be a favor for a friend."

Bolan realized how hollow his explanation sounded.

Wilson's skeptical expression showed the soldier that his doubts were much the same.

"I doubt if Sacco knows exactly who his friends are today."

Bolan smiled thinly.

"It's an occupational hazard."

"I guess. Where can I get in touch with you?"

"I'm in and out," the warrior told him vaguely. "I'll call you tomorrow if my people turn up something you could use."

"Appreciate it."

But Bob Wilson's tone conveyed a different feeling. Clearly, the detective still thought he was being frozen out of some clandestine operation at the federal level. He might well make a call to check it out, start probing on his own but it was a risk Mack Bolan would have to live with. In any case the worst that could happen would be Wilson's discovery that he was not, in fact, employed by Justice.

There were a host of other problems, each more pressing, on the soldier's mind and he dismissed the risk as minimal. His cover was expendable; its violation would not put the Metro man one step closer to caging the Executioner. If anything, it would only serve to deepen the confusion he was operating under now.

They shook hands grimly, mourners parting at the funeral of a mutual friend. As Bolan made his way back to the dark unmarked sedan he could feel Wilson's eyes following him across the grassy shoulder of the road and past the bullet-riddled Chevy that had been a coffin for Hannon and Evangelina moments earlier. By the time he reached the car and risked a backward glance, however, Wilson was deep in conversation with some of his officers.

Bolan fired the engine, powered out of there with gravel spitting from his tires. He put a mile behind him before he permitted his mind to attack the question of who had killed John Hannon and the woman.

It was a question he would have to answer in his own best interests if he planned to keep on breathing long enough to finish what he had started in Miami. He owed that much to Hannon, to the woman, yes, and he would see through what the two of them had begun before he arrived.

The worst had come to pass. Two more lives on Bolan's soul, joining the others that dated back into the infancy of his private war against the Mafia. Two sisters now, and Bolan knew with agonizing certainty that he would never wipe their faces from his memory, not if he lived a thousand years.

And it was time for him to spread a little of the agony, the hell, around Miami, right. Sharing time for damn sure.

The Executioner had a list in mind, and someone on that roster knew precisely what had happened here today and why. Mack Bolan had to have that knowledge, now, before his campaign could proceed another step toward resolution.

There would be time enough for getting even when he had the targets sorted out and cataloged, all neatly organized for mass destruction.

He was looking forward to the coming judgment day, right.

But first he had to get in touch with Toro.

If it was not too late already.

19

Bolan pulled his car into a scenic turnout off Ocean Drive and parked facing the Atlantic. Out beyond the beach the water was already dark, forbidding in its vastness. At his back, behind the skyline of Miami, a tropical sunset was burning out in hues of pink and lavender. In his rearview mirror, the dying rays glinted off the hustling cars that flowed along the drive.

He sat there, smoking, glancing frequently at his wristwatch, a loaded Ingram MAC-10 submachine gun on the seat beside him. There was no such thing, he knew, as being overcautious these days in Miami. Not when half the underworld was working overtime to find and kill you.

The Executioner was more than ready when the Cadillac turned off, separating smoothly from the flow of traffic, headlights dancing as the driver guided her carefully over a series of speed bumps. The glare of headlights momentarily filled his rearview and Bolan averted his eyes, concentrating on the side mirror now. He stubbed out his smoke in the dashboard ashtray, then casually reached for the Ingram, lifting it into his lap. He kept one hand around the stubby weapon's pistol grip and watched as the Caddy rolled into an empty parking space beside him on the passenger's side.

The other driver killed his lights and engine, remained

seated behind the wheel and stared straight ahead. Inside the Caddy other faces were turning to examine Bolan now, checking out his car and the surroundings, hesitant, cautious.

The car was ten years old, reminiscent of a bygone era. Somehow it seemed to fit its occupants that way. They, too, were out of sync with history, living anachronisms who refused to compromise with changing times. They reminded Bolan of the samurai, devoted to a code of honor; a military life-style that had become passé to everyone around them.

Still they carried on the fight and Bolan felt for them, aware in his heart that their own unending battle was as hopeless as his own.

It had taken several calls to make connections with El Toro and arrange the meeting.

A back door on the Caddy opened, and one of the gunners inside covered the dome light with his palm as Toro climbed out. Glancing around at the night, he crossed to Bolan's car and got in, sparing a look for the Ingram clutched in the Executioner's lap. Toro settled into the passenger seat and closed the door behind him.

"How goes the rattling of cages?" he asked.

"It goes. And you?"

"I traced Raoul's lieutenant." Toro flashed a little conspiratorial smile. "He was reluctant to confide in me at first. I had to be quite harsh with him."

Mack Bolan knew how harsh the Latin *soldado* could be, and he could almost sympathize with Ornelas's second-in-command. Almost, right, but not quite. He waited silently for Toro to continue in his own way and time.

"You still have interest in this Jose 99?"

Mack Bolan felt the involuntary prickling of his scalp.

"I do."

Toro paused briefly, then said, "He is Raoul."

And Bolan saw a couple of the pieces fall together, snapping soundly into place. He recalled the words of Captain Wilson as they stood together at the scene of Hannon and Evangelina's murder.

"The FBI says it has something on him from a routine wiretap on the Cuban embassy. He calls the cultural attaché there from time to time."

Then Bolan replied, "I see."

The Cuban raised an eyebrow.

"You are not surprised?"

"Let's say it fits."

He briefed Toro quickly on what Wilson had told him, and the Cuban's face was going through some changes of its own as he digested Bolan's words. When the Executioner had finished speaking Toro made a disgusted face.

"I underestimated this one's treachery," he said.

He spent a moment staring out across the beach at darkened water, watching the moon rise.

"This cultural attaché that you speak of, Jorge Ybarra, he is DGI."

Bolan stiffened even though he wasn't surprised to hear what he had already begun to suspect. Still, he was angry at himself for not putting the pieces together sooner, in time to save a few good lives along the way.

The DGI, of course. Castro's secret service—basically a Spanish-speaking adjunct of the KGB.

It fit, damn right.

It fit too well.

"Raoul has the trucks and weapons that your friend is looking for," Toro said absently. "Raoul is responsible for stealing them."

Bolan resisted an urge to put John Hannon in the past tense, to tell Toro all about Evangelina. They were running on the numbers, and every second counted now. There was no time to waste in agonizing over battle casualties.

"For weeks now," Toro continued, "this *pendejo* has recruited gunmen. Omega 7 hides them, but they have a special mission. I believed it was Raoul, but now I see that there is more."

"What mission?" Bolan prodded.

"Key Biscayne."

Something turned over sluggishly in Bolan's gut, but he held himself in check, waiting for Toro to continue.

When the Cuban spoke again his voice was emotionless as he began to spell it out.

"One truck filled with explosives, to blow the causeway, *sí?* Three, four others with the *marielistas,* weapons. All in position early while the people are asleep."

And Toro did not have to say any more. Mack Bolan had the picture clearly in his mind, and any way he looked at it, it came out as a bloodbath in the streets.

"When do they move?"

"Tomorrow. Dawn."

The warrior felt a headache start to throb behind his eyes and raised one hand briefly to massage his temples, clearing his mind for what lay ahead.

"We've got a lot to do," he said simply.

Toro turned to face him, his features lost in shadow inside the sedan's darkened interior. His deep voice seemed to emerge from a bottomless pit.

"My men are working on Raoul," he said. "I'll have him soon, I think."

Bolan nodded curtly.

"Okay. He's yours. I have some stops to make. We'd better synchronize."

"Agreed."

They spent the next quarter hour laying plans for the approaching battle. It was completely dark by the time they went their different ways. A darkness of the soul as much as anything.

It captured Bolan's killing mood precisely, as he pushed the rental car through Stygian blackness, following the coastline, with the wild, untameable Atlantic on his right-hand side.

In his heart the warrior knew that the only way to drive the darkness back was with a purifying flame, bright and fiercely hot enough to send the cannibals scuttling back underground where they belonged.

He had the fire inside him now, and he was primed to let it out, to strike a spark that might consume Miami in the end, before it burned away to ashes.

The Executioner was carrying his torch into the darkness.

20

The raid on Key Biscayne made ghoulish sense to Bolan. As a master tactician himself, he could appreciate the plotters' strategic perception. It was a tight plan, well-conceived, immensely practical despite its loony overtones.

Like something from a madman's nightmares, right. But this nightmare was coming true tomorrow in broad daylight.

The fact that it was clearly suicidal for the troops involved meant nothing. The planners would be counting on high casualties, and every man they lost before the final curtain would be one less talking mouth to help police backtrack along the bloody trail of conspiracy. Whatever happened to the shock troops once they were engaged, there would be time enough for them to wreak bloody havoc in the streets before the last of them could be eradicated by a counterforce.

Time enough to orchestrate a massacre, damned right, and throw Miami's affluent society into a screaming panic.

Hell, it was almost perfect.

Bolan did not spare more than a passing thought to motives in the plot. In the end, it mattered little whether Raoul Ornelas was an opportunist seeking ransom for himself, a dedicated rightist striking back somehow at

Castro and America, or a turncoat working hand in glove with Cuban agents. Whichever way it cut—a hostage situation or a random massacre—the end result, inevitably, had to be a bloodbath.

Ornelas was committing criminals and addicts, all the human dregs that he could muster, as his front-line troops. There was no way on earth that he could hope to rein them in once they had scented blood. Ornelas *had* to know that much, and from that grisly certainty, Mack Bolan knew a massacre was what Jose 99 had planned from the beginning.

The DGI and its controllers in the KGB would profit doubly from the holocaust. The chaos, killing, violence—the goals of global terrorism—all of these were ends in themselves, but there were greater potentials there.

Supposing that Ornelas was exposed, revealed in court and through the press as the mastermind of the plot, it would, if handled carefully, reflect upon the anti-Castro movement rather than upon the Communists who hatched the plot. The end result, disgrace for any Cuban exiles who were militant or even vocal in their opposition to the current Havana regime, would bring oppressive crackdowns at the state and federal level, doubling security for Castro at no expense to the Cuban government itself. Castro's chief enemies in the United States would be surveilled, perhaps incarcerated...and years would pass before the anti-Castro movement won back any small degree of visible respectability.

Mack Bolan, at the moment, had no interest in the politics involved. His mind was on the countless lives that would be lost unless he found a way to short-circuit the plan in its initial stages.

Geography and economics helped the terrorists select their target. Key Biscayne's sixty-three hundred affluent residents lived on an island barely four square miles in area. A former U.S. President maintained his winter White House there, but nowadays the majority of tourists headed straight for Bill Baggs Cape Florida State Park, to see the historic lighthouse. And they came in whopping numbers, right.

Key Biscayne connected to the mainland by a single causeway—and its demolition as described by Toro would destroy it, or at least render it impassable for hours, even days. With that route cut, relief would have to come by water or by air...and either way, relief troops would be landing in the face of hostile guns once terrorists controlled the island.

Bolan knew that if the terrorists gained a beachhead on Biscayne, there would be no stopping them before they had a chance to wreak their vengeance on a sleepy populace.

If possible, Bolan and the troops that Toro might be able to recruit had to stop the juggernaut before it started bearing down upon its target.

So far, the Executioner was hampered by a lack of battlefield intel. He did not know the number of his enemies, their firepower or their precise location. Every piece of information that he lacked made it more likely that the small defensive force would fail.

But the very things that made Biscayne a tempting target also worked in Bolan's favor. Using trucks for transport, the invaders were restricted to a single avenue of entry to the island: over Rickenbacker Causeway to Virginia Key, then over Bear Cut Causeway to the killing ground itself on Key Biscayne. With that in mind,

Mack Bolan could map out the different approaches to the causeway, narrow down the hostiles' route to half a dozen possibilities.

And then what?

By himself or with Grimaldi flying cover, even with the guns that Toro might be able to recruit, he could not cover all of the approaches with sufficient force to turn an armed brigade around. The roadblock must be inconspicuous enough to slip past the notice of police, yet strong enough to stop the killer convoy cold, without allowing even one of them to reach the target zone.

Clearly, Bolan needed reinforcements in a hurry.

The sudden inspiration struck him, and it was simplicity itself.

Suddenly he knew exactly what he had to do and where to find the reinforcements that he needed. It would require audacity and nerve—two qualities the Executioner possessed in abundance—but if Bolan could pull it off he might be able to bring down two vultures with a single shot.

All he had to do was change identities again in midstride, without losing his momentum. Just a simple probe inside the enemy encampment, right.

That, and then get out again intact, with time to spare before he had to meet the final strike on Key Biscayne.

A simple matter, right.

No sweat.

Except that he could lose it anywhere along the way, with one false step.

And if he lost it...then he would die along with others, and the savages would breeze through unobstructed to their target area. There would be hours or days of mayhem.

Mac Bolan pushed the thought out of his mind and concentrated on his actions of the next few moments.

Defeat was not an acceptable alternative.

He would have victory, or death in the attempt. And if he died, a lot of savage souls were going with him.

21

Phillip Sacco did not have his usual nightmare on the night after Omega's visit. You have to sleep in order to have nightmares, and for the aging *capo,* sleep was suddenly in very short supply. For the first time in his adult life he doubted his ability to control his own environment.

And it was a frightening sensation.

After twenty-four hours he still hadn't been able to get a line on Tommy Drake's assassins. Omega was out there, but Sacco's calls to New York City, Chicago and the West Coast had been unable to confirm or deny the black ace's standing with *La Commissione.* And worst of all, Sacco's town was blowing up around him, dreadful rumors circulating.

Rumors about marksman's medals, damn right, and stories that Mack The Bastard Bolan might be back in town, goddamnit.

Now *there* was a recurring nightmare—one that Sacco could not seem to wake himself up from no matter how he tried.

Phil Sacco had been convinced, like all of his *amici* in the honored society of Mafia, that Bolan had finally died in his New York flame-out some time back. It had not been smooth sailing with him gone, of course; he left the brotherhood in an unholy shambles when he

faded from the scene, and there had been a recent wave
of state and federal offensives—but anything was better
than going to bed with the fear that you might not wake
up in the morning.

Anything was better, sure, than jumping every time a
shadow moved around you, any time a man in black
might cross your path.

Anything, yeah, except maybe not sleeping at all.

If Mack Bolan was back, Sacco told himself, the
frigging guy had made a critical mistake by coming back
to southern Florida right now.

Phil Sacco meant to see that Bolan paid for this
mistake with his life.

The telephone in his study started ringing, but Sacco
did not answer it. He waited while Solly Cusamano, the
houseman, took care of it, picking it up on the third
ring.

Sacco figured that any call at this hour of the night
just had to be bad news—unless, perhaps, it might be
one of his hunter crews reporting with information on
the bums who took down Tommy Drake.

There was a long moment's delay, then Solly knocked
on the door of his study, poking his head in at Sacco's
summons. Cusamano looked worried and apologetic.

"It's that Omega, boss. You wanna talk to him?"

Sacco stared at the silent telephone for a moment,
allowing himself the luxury of pretending that he had a
choice.

"I'll take it, yeah. Thanks, Solly."

Cusamano ducked back out and closed the door behind him. Sacco lifted the telephone receiver, listening
silently until the houseman hung up on the other
extension.

"Okay."

The black ace's voice came back at him across the line, deep and graveyard cold.

"I'm glad to hear your voice, Phil."

"Yeah?"

Omega chuckled, making a reptilian hissing sound.

"I had an idea I might be too late."

"Too late for what?"

Sacco did not try to hide the irritation that was slowly creeping into his voice.

"To say goodbye," the ace responded.

Irritation blossomed into full-blown anger now.

"It's too damned late for playing games," the *capo* snapped.

"You're wising up."

"Goddammit—"

Omega did not raise his voice, but still his words managed to override Sacco's outburst.

"Tommy Drake was pissing on you, Phil. He was setting you up."

"That's bullshit."

But the doubt was planted in his mind now. Sacco had lived too long in the Mafia's paranoid jungle to automatically rule out any treason, any treachery.

"You know he was connected with the Cubans," Omega responded, sounding almost disinterested. "Do you know what they were working on?"

"Of course, I knew," he blustered, bluffing. "What kind of question—"

"Then you know about the move on Key Biscayne."

There was momentary silence on both ends of the line, Sacco racking his brain, loathe to admit ignorance, but coming up with nothing that made sense.

Omega went ahead without his answer, reading everything he had to know into the *capo's* strained silence.

"It's a psycho proposition, Phil. The feeling is your boy came up with it to pacify the Cubans. On the side, he's had them laying trails that lead right back to you."

Sacco's hand was white-knuckled now on the receiver, so tight his hand was shaking.

"I . . . guess I don't know what you mean."

And Omega told him a horror story, speaking in dry, clipped tones, the weight of his words bearing down into the leather-upholstered cushions of his easy chair. When he heard it all, Omega offered him an out, explained how he could save it—part of it, at any rate—if he moved quickly and decisively enough.

"You think that you can handle all that, Phil?"

Sacco scowled at the receiver in his hand, hating the man at the other end, hating Tommy Drake for putting him in this untenable position.

"I'll handle it, all right."

"I hope so. Everybody's counting on you."

Sacco stiffened, knowing the reverse side of the coin. *Everybody's waiting to see you screw up; waiting to divide your operations when you're dead and buried.*

"Tell them that it's in the bag."

Omega hung up on him without another word, and Sacco cradled the receiver briefly, glaring at it, not moving his hand. Then he lifted it again and started dialing rapidly.

Sacco was calling in the troops, damn right.

And the *capo mafioso* of Miami did not have a lot of time to lose.

CAPTAIN ROBERT WILSON drained the last few dregs of coffee from his mug and pushed it away from him across the cluttered desk. He rocked back in his swivel chair, stretching, deliberately closing his eyes as he turned toward the clock on the wall, refusing to acknowledge the hour and how little he had achieved this night in concrete terms.

Beyond the glass partition that contained his private office, a skeleton crew was manning the Homicide squad room on the graveyard shift. The hackneyed gag was often used to get a laugh from officers in Homicide, but Wilson did not feel a bit like laughing at the moment.

The first reports of Hannon's death were open on the desk in front of him. He could recite them almost word for word by now and still they told him nothing.

Everything was there, of course, in terms of the procedures. Ballistics and trajectories, points of entry and exit. Wilson knew precisely how John Hannon died, and he had a fair idea of who was responsible. . . but none of it had put him any closer to solution of the crime.

He had pursued LaMancha's lead on the dead girl and struck surprising pay dirt at the federal building. Her name had been Evangelina, and her file at Justice had included information on familial relations—on a sister, in particular.

Deceased.

And *that* had been a shocker, goddamned right. It raised some ghosts for Wilson, dating back to other days when Hannon was the captain, and a soldier newly home from Vietnam was settling a family score against the Mafia. The Bolan hunt had been an education in itself; it showed Robert Wilson a side of Hannon—and a side of himself—that he had never quite suspected.

A side that, yeah, could be damned frightening at times.

And Wilson had not overlooked the ominous parallels between that other time of killing and his present situation.

One sister, Margarita, murdered by the syndicate the first time Bolan was in town; the other ambushed now, with Hannon, just when someone had been knocking over mob concessions, leaving marksman's medals as a calling card.

Not *someone,* Bob Wilson corrected himself. It was Mack Bolan. He was still alive, somehow, against the odds. It was confirmed by FBI and press reports.

The bastard was alive and he was back, no doubt about it. And he was Wilson's responsibility this time.

The telephone jangled on his desk and Wilson grabbed for it absentmindedly, his thoughts still focused on his problem of the moment as he answered.

"Captain Wilson, Homicide."

"You're working late."

He recognized Frank LaMancha's voice although they had spoken only once before. There was something in the tonal quality that sent a little chill along his spine.

"I've got a lot to do," he answered.

"You'd better wrap it up. The curtain's coming down."

"That right?"

There was skepticism in the homicide detective's voice, but he tempered it with caution.

"Bet on it. Sacco and Ornelas are about to tangle. You'll want to be there."

Wilson searched around in the debris heaped upon his desk, finally coming up with a pencil and note pad.

"Where and when?"

"Not yet," LaMancha told him. "We need to let this run its course."

"I see."

The image in his mind was grisly, littered with the dead and dying.

"You're telling me a shooting war's about to break, and asking me to sit on it."

"You won't be missing anything, unless you try to put the lid on prematurely."

"Better I should wait until the county morgue is standing room only? It doesn't work that way around Miami, mister."

"Easy, Captain. All I'm saying is that you could blow it if you get too eager."

"Maybe that's a chance I'll have to take."

"I don't. Goodbye."

Wilson felt a sudden rush, akin to panic, as he saw his chance begin to slip away.

"Hold on there, dammit! I'm still listening."

The "federal agent's" voice was cautious in its own right now.

"No specifics yet. You'll have to trust me."

"That's a rare commodity." Wilson hesitated, thinking it over briefly. "I'd like to take a look at what I'm walking into."

"Fair enough."

LaMancha briefed him quickly, sticking to the basics, but it was enough to put a sour taste in Wilson's mouth and set his stomach rolling. Suddenly, from out of nowhere, he had a hunch that blossomed into inspiration, revelation.

LaMancha was about to hang up, and the captain blurted out, "Hey, Mack!"

A heartbeat's hesitation, barely noticeable, on the other end of the line.

"The name's still Frank."

"Oh. . .right." Wilson suddenly felt foolish, asinine. "Uh. . .listen. . .thanks for the tip, okay?"

"No sweat. Just don't be late."

The line went dead and Wilson cradled his receiver, puzzling over his hunch for a moment, finally dismissing it. He set about his business, waking people and making sure they would be exactly where he needed them, precisely when their services were called for.

Like Phil Sacco on the other side of town, Bob Wilson was calling in his forces, right, preparing for a good old-fashioned shooting war.

Toro's driver braked the Cadillac beneath some trees, partially sheltering the car from the nearest streetlight. Inside the car the faces of his troops were lost in shadows.

It was almost dawn, and yet the sunrise had not touched the northern part of Miami. It lingered on the ocean, painting beaches gray, then pink and gold, finally creeping in past the beachfront hotels, and only then descending on the residential districts with its warming touch, bringing the world to life.

This morning, in the vanguard of the dawn, Toro and his men had come not with life, but with death in their hearts. They were on a military mission and the setting made no difference, tactically, to their procedures or their goals.

They had come for Raoul Ornelas, and they would have him, or all six of them would die in the attempt.

The target was a ranch-style home in a fashionable

part of the North Miami suburb. Sitting in the Caddy
with a weapon in his lap, Toro reflected bitterly that
Ornelas had not only betrayed the cause but he had also
physically deserted his people, putting himself beyond
their reach from the stews of Little Havana. Ornelas
was a man apart, attempting to eke out a place for himself above the battle.

But this day, El Toro meant to bring him down.

The place was built for status and appearances instead of defense. A six-foot decorative wall surrounded
the acre of grounds, and the house was set well back
behind a manicured lawn, partially screened by trees.
But this was not a fortress. They could encounter
danger there, even death, but not before they made their
way inside.

In seconds, all of them had left the Cadillac and
scaled the wall, regrouping in the shadows and waiting
for instructions from their leader. Toro went through all
of it again, to be on the safe side, substituting hand
gestures for words whenever possible, keeping his eyes
and ears alert for the danger of dogs or watchmen.

He had deliberately timed the raid to coincide with
sunrise, from knowledge of Ornelas's plans for the
morning, and because the early morning brought a
natural sluggishness to men on watch. A sentry's
natural defenses lagged at sunrise, and with his meager
force behind him, Toro knew he could use every single
advantage available.

Ornelas had sentries posted, but they were all immediately around the house, and they were not alert
enough to save themselves from death as it came creeping toward them through the morning mist.

Toro and his five warriors fanned out, moving low

and fast across the lawn like silent shadows, gliding in the face of sunrise, closing on the house with lightning strides.

Emiliano took one sentry with his silenced Ruger automatic. One shot, with the bulky suppressor almost touching the base of the target's skull, and the little .22-caliber round cored through bone and muscle, clipping the stem of the brain.

Toro made the second kill himself, slipping a noose of piano wire over a young man's head and bringing it tight around his throat. The wire bit deep, cutting off his wind and releasing a Niagara of blood as the soldier struggled briefly in Toro's grasp, finally relaxing into death.

Toro's group circled back around the house, encountering no more resistance, and they found a service entrance in the rear. Ornelas was coming up in the world, the Cuban warrior thought. High time that someone put him back in touch with the grim realities of their unending war for freedom.

In a war you executed traitors, yes. But sometimes, given opportunity, a trial could be instructive.

They pushed on through the service entrance, barging into a combination kitchen and pantry with Juanito leading, his Uzi probing out ahead of him and seeking targets. He found them in the kitchen, three more pistoleros, chowing down on breakfast prior to relieving their comrades on the outside watch.

In the heartbeat before everything exploded into chaos, Toro recognized one of the men, a former follower who had defected to Ornelas, seduced by his promises of action and material rewards.

The guards were digging for sidearms, fanning out

quickly, professionally. Juanito snarled and held the trigger down on his little Israeli stuttergun, raking the kitchen from left to right and back again, riddling pots and pans, puncturing the microwave oven and refrigerator with 9mm parabellum rounds.

He caught one of the guards retreating through a connecting doorway, helped him get there with a blazing figure eight that split his spine and blew him away. A second figure was peeling off to the left, crouching behind the dining table as he brought a gun to bear upon the small invasion force, but he was not quite fast enough. Another Uzi burst removed his face with something less than surgical precision, scattering his brains across a wall.

The third man actually got a shot off before the weapons of all six invaders bore down on him, opening fire as one and blowing him backward, a riddled, leaking straw man suddenly devoid of any life.

They swept on past the human ruins, robbed of their surprise advantage now, knowing that they might run into anything beyond the pantry door. What Toro had not quite expected was the sumptuous living room, complete with curving staircase leading to the upper floor and bedrooms. Everything was hardwood, dark, crushed velvet, carpet deep enough to hide in if you bellied down.

A shotgun boomed its greeting from the stairs, and Toro's squad scattered, going to ground behind the ornate pieces of furniture. Mano was slow, and the second shotgun blast caught him in midstride, lifting him off his feet and spinning him around before dumping him facedown on the carpeting. He was dead before he hit the floor, and from his place of bare concealment, Toro could already see the small *soldado's* lifeblood soaking down into the nylon shag.

Above them and across the room, the shotgunner was getting overconfident. He showed himself, looking for another target. It was his last mistake. Toro raised the .45 he carried, sighting quickly down the slide and squeezing off a double punch, even as Juanito stroked a burst out of his lethal Uzi from the other side of the room.

The shotgunner was crucified to the wall, leaving long streaked traces of himself as he slid away, finally coming down head over heels, landing in an untidy heap at the foot of the staircase.

Toro and his survivors took the stairs in a rush, mounting them swiftly. They were alert to danger, but the final gunner took them by surprise, looming around the corner of the second-story landing, banging away almost in their faces with the nickel-plated revolver that he carried.

Juanito took a round between the eyes, another in the Adam's apple, dead before his trigger finger clenched, unloading the Uzi's magazine in one last, long ragged burst. He took the gunner with him, riddling the man right where he stood and sweeping him away. His job completed, little Juanito collapsed facedown on the risers, his Uzi trapped beneath his lifeless body as he fell.

They took the bedrooms one by one, crashing each in turn until they reached what was clearly the master's room. Toro gave the door a flying kick and they edged back from the open portal, waiting for a burst of fire that never came.

The room was empty, rumpled bed and scattered nightclothes bearing testimony to the fact that their quarry had been there only moments earlier. Without speaking, El Toro began a rapid search of the room, looking under the bed, into the adjoining marble bath, moving out onto the veranda that overlooked a swimming pool in back.

Nothing.

The Cuban commando was frowning as he reentered the bedroom, but his expression changed at once when he beheld the folding closet doors. Moving swiftly across to stand in front of the closet, he raised the .45 autoloader, braced it in both hands and pumped three rounds waist high across the double doors.

It was a gamble, but his aim was true. A strangled little cry from inside the depths of the closet rewarded him, and Toro closed the gap, flinging the door wide, no longer afraid that Ornelas would pose any physical threat to his men.

The traitor was crouched in a corner of the closet, hidden in among perhaps fifty expensive-looking suits. And Toro did not have to ask himself where the money for these clothes, this house, had come from. Ornelas had sold his people and his honor, sold himself to the highest bidder like a *puta* on the street...and it was time for him to begin paying his dues.

Toro leaned inside the closet, grabbed a handful of his quarry's hair and dragged him out into the middle of the room. Ornelas was sniveling, crying now, a man afraid of death when it came calling at his door. He looked from one face to the other, always coming back to Toro, still afraid to speak although he plainly longed to beg for mercy.

Toro did the talking for him.

"Stand up, Raoul," he snapped. "It's time to meet your people."

22

Don Phillip Sacco shifted restlessly in the back seat of the silver Rolls. Sacco wanted a cigar, but he was afraid his hands would shake if he tried to light one. He would do anything to stifle the urge rather than let his soldiers see his nervousness on the eve of battle. So he settled down to wait for the word that would propel him into combat like some kind of junior hit man.

There were six guns with him in the Rolls: one on either side of him in the back, a pair on the jump seats, and a couple more in the front. All of them were armed to the teeth, their hands held close to holstered hardware, itching for a chance to use it. They were primed to kill, damn right, and wanting it so bad that they could taste it.

They were good boys, these *amici*. Some of them were younger than he might have liked, but all the seasoned guns were gone or out to pasture these days. Soldiering was actually a young man's business, anyhow, he thought, although an old horse like himself could still teach them a thing or two when it came to kicking ass.

The coal-black Lincoln Continentals parked on either side of Sacco's Rolls contained identical contingents of his hardmen—eighteen guns in all. It was the core of his strike force, and they had been waiting in the parking lot outside an all-night supermarket now for the better part of ninety minutes, looking for word from one of the point cars as soon as that first crucial contact with the enemy was made.

Sacco was the general this time out, and he would not be hiding somewhere behind the lines, no way. He was intent on leading his troops into battle, closing the bottleneck with his enemies trapped inside.

It was an easy stand, there being only three main routes approaching Rickenbacker Causeway. And no matter which direction the Cuban gunners came from, they would have to choose one of the routes that Sacco had already picketed with lookouts at strategic locations.

Any way they came he had them, and his own central location made it feasible for him to instantly respond to any contact point within moments of the initial sighting.

The plan was simple, and that was why he liked it.

Sacco did not fully understand what Tommy Drake had been doing with his Cuban contacts, and at the moment he did not really give a damn. The time had come to square accounts, for damn sure.

Time to save some face and put his house in order, right, and regain some of his slipping prestige with the commission.

When he had finished whipping ass today there would be time enough to look around and see how far the treason had spread within his family. Time enough, perhaps, to show a certain smart-assed Ace of Spades how the old pros handled revolutions in the ranks.

A walkie-talkie crackled into life between the front-seat gunners. Sacco snapped his fingers, reaching for the radio and taking it from the driver's hand.

"This is Digger, calling home base. You there, Chief?"

Sacco recognized it as his scout on Brickell Avenue.

"I'm listening," he snapped. "What is it?"

"Four vans headed your way, Cubans driving."

"Slow 'em down the best you can. We're coming in."

"You got it, boss."

Sacco held the transmission button down, calling in the other point cars, knowing that he would need every gun he had.

"All cars, form up on number three's position. North on Brickell. Move it!"

He did not wait for their responses. His driver was already peeling out of the parking lot. The gunners all around him were unlimbering their weapons, checking loads.

The *capo* reached under his jacket and slipped the stainless .45 AMT Hardballer out of side leather. He drew back the slide to chamber a live one, easing the hammer down with the ball of his thumb.

It had been years since he had fired a shot in anger, but he had not lost the touch, hell no. He'd teach these kids a thing or two, starting now.

There was virtually no traffic on Brickell Avenue as the three-car caravan pushed north, the Rolls leading, and it only took them moments to reach their destination. Sacco had no trouble picking out the target zone from three long blocks away.

The Digger's Caddy crew wagon was parked diagonally across two lanes, the gunners crouched behind it, already firing over hood and trunk in the direction of some stationary vans. One of the troops was stretched out dead on the asphalt, a blood slick expanding gradually around him.

Beyond the Caddy three trucks were stalled in the

middle of the street, with Cubans spilling out, deploying under fire. A fourth truck was parked at an angle that indicated it had tried to swing around the Caddy, but the shattered windshield and leaking radiator bore mute testimony to the fury of the fusillade that stopped it dead.

Phil Sacco's caravan screeched to a halt behind the Cadillac, the reinforcements piling out, already under fire from the enemy as they moved into position. Sacco's aging bones protested as he ran, trying to keep his head down and out of the line of fire.

He reached the sanctuary of the Cadillac and found a place beside the crew chief, Digger Fontenelli. Sacco risked a glance over the roof of the limo, almost losing his nose as a bullet caromed off the bodywork inches from his face. After that, he was more circumspect in seeking an angle on the fray.

The Caddy was taking repeated hits, rocking to the tempo of the incoming automatic fire. There seemed to be a hundred guns against them, and Sacco was already having second thoughts about the wisdom of his plan, engaging the hostiles this way in broad daylight, where the cops or Feds or anybody might drop in at any moment.

To hell with it. They were in the middle of it now, and there was only one way out: directly through the enemy, right on.

The Digger straightened up, angling for a shot with his stubby riot shotgun, and a sniper picked him off, putting a parabellum round right through his left eye socket, taking out the whole back of his skull in a soggy crimson spray. His body tumbled backward, hitting the asphalt with a sound of grim finality.

Sacco reacted quickly, the age-old reflexes taking over as he rose to his full height, the stainless .45 seeking a target. He spied the rifleman who dropped the Digger, and Sacco squeezed off a single booming round that picked the Cuban off his feet and slammed him back against the fender of the nearest moving van.

More incoming rounds drove the *capo* back under cover, but his pulse was racing now. He was excited by the proximity of death, the high-altitude rush of having spilled blood.

Another gunner toppled to his right, draped across the Caddy's hood, his pistol clattering on the pavement. Sacco saw his own chauffeur go down, blood pumping from a ragged throat wound, gasping out his life while those around him went about their business, killing and being killed in turn.

And suddenly, the adrenaline high was turning into fear. The *capo* saw that they were hopelessly outnumbered, losing ground. There was no way in hell that they could hope to take the Cubans out and get away intact.

A tire exploded on the Caddy, then another, and Sacco crouched lower for protection. He listened to the bullets drumming into the bodywork now like rain on a tin roof, threatening to break through and find him on the other side at any moment.

He fought down an urge to cut and run for the safety of his armored Rolls. He had no driver now, could not be heard above the din of gunfire, and it suddenly occurred to him that he could no longer call off the battle even if he wanted to.

And he did want to, more than he could comprehend through the panic fogging his mind.

He half rose from his combat crouch, prepared to order anyone within earshot to retreat and make for the other cars, but before he could speak, a big gun opened up from the sidelines, filling the air with its thunder.

Sacco actually saw its projectile strike the rearmost moving van and suddenly the truck erupted, disintegrating at the seams and shooting everything inside into a towering inferno. Smoke, flames and shrapnel were heavenbound and bodies were flying, some of them flattened by the concussion.

Shock waves rocked the Caddy and Sacco stumbled, sprawling on his face. The stainless .45 spun out of his hand, and before he could recover it, there was another sharp explosion, and another, seeming to walk along the line of moving vans, closing in on his own exposed position.

Someone close to him was screaming, a sound of blind, unreasoning panic in the midst of hell on earth. And it took the *capo* of Miami several endless heartbeats to realize that the shrieking voice was his own.

MACK BOLAN WAS FLYING the skywatch with Grimaldi, circling high above the Rickenbacker Causeway in their Bell executive whirlybird, heading inland. Their radio was set to eavesdrop on the frequency employed by Phillip Sacco's walkie-talkies, waiting for the word that would confirm some contact with the enemy.

Riding shotgun beside Grimaldi, Bolan was rigged for hellfire. He was dressed in tiger-stripe fatigues, outfitted in military webbing with the sleek Beretta underneath his left arm and the silver AutoMag in place on his right hip. He held the XM-18 40mm grenade launcher in his lap; the bandoliers crossing his chest were filled with alternating HE, smoke and antipersonnel rounds, touch-coordinated for easy access in the heat of combat.

They were skimming in across the long deserted beach when the radio hissed into life.

"This is Digger, calling home base. You there, chief?"

"I'm listening. What is it?"

"Four vans headed your way, Cubans driving."

"Slow 'em down the best you can. We're coming in."

"You got it, boss."

A brief hesitation, and when the commanding voice resumed, there was no mistaking Sacco's intonation.

"All cars, form up on number three's position. North on Brickell. Move it!"

Bolan glanced over quickly at Grimaldi and the pilot nodded, banking the chopper, homing in on Brickell Avenue and following its course along the shoreline. Within moments they had sighted the little convoy, the silver Rolls leading two Lincolns. Way back, just joining the parade but moving fast to make up time, two other crew wagons were trailing, pulling in the flanks.

Forty gunners, Bolan guessed, maybe more if they were packed in like sardines. The Executioner wondered how many Cubans it would take to fill three moving vans, leaving the fourth one empty except for its lethal cargo of explosives. Any way he counted it, the totals came up spelling bloodbath.

They skimmed over the skirmish lines where a black Caddy had the four trucks blocked and troops had already engaged each other on the street. Grimaldi swung wide, looking for a clean LZ, finally bringing Bolan in from behind a little shopping mall that fronted the street.

The ace flier hovered five or six feet above the flat roof of a Laundromat and Bolan flashed a thumbs-up prior to jumping. He landed on the run, ducking beneath the rotor wash to take up his position at the front edge of the roof, overlooking the battlefield some fifty yards away.

After discharging his passenger, Grimaldi lifted off and took position in the rafters, out of small-arms range. At need, he could get in touch with Bolan by means of a tiny transceiver headpiece that the warrior had included in his battle dress.

The reinforcements had arrived as Bolan reached his lookout post, and now gunners were spilling out of the assorted crew wagons, the Rolls and carbon-copy Continentals, trading fire with the scattered Cubans. From where he stood, Mack Bolan could make out the bobbing, weaving figure of Phil Sacco as he looked for cover down behind the makeshift roadblock formed by the bullet-punctured Cadillac.

He let them get to know each other for moment, watching troopers fall on either side, looking for the best angle of attack for himself. Finally, he decided that the Cubans would most likely have their explosives stashed in the rearmost van, for safety's sake, and also making it easier to shut down the causeway behind the three troop carriers.

He raised the XM-18 launcher and announced his entry to the battle with an HE round that impacted on the rearmost moving van. A secondary blast tore the early-morning scene apart. It was a thunderous explosion, shattering windows for half a mile along the boulevard, leveling every upright body on the battlefield with a massive shock wave that rocked the other vans and vehicles, deafening the participants and leaving them shaken, stunned.

The small arms fire below him dried out completely for a moment following the blast, and Bolan moved into the breach, his projectile launcher belching fire and smoke as he picked out new targets, walking the HE rounds along the line of makeshift troop vehicles. The vans were going up like a string of giant firecrackers, scattering their occupants in bits and pieces, driving the survivors in a frantic scramble-search for any cover that might save them from the rain of fire.

He pivoted and dropped another high-explosive can directly onto Sacco's silver Rolls, consuming it in fire and smoke that quickly spread to take the Caddy out as well. Below him all was chaos now, the gunners on both sides unloading aimlessly, none of them apparently pinpointing the source of their sudden disaster.

Bolan's HE rounds were spent, but he kept on firing, scattering the shaken, stunned survivors with round after punishing round of buckshot, blowing ragged holes in the disintegrating ranks, ripping flesh and fabric at the limit of his howitzer's effective range. There was no answering fire, and by the time he exhausted his first drum it was apparent to the soldier that none would be forthcoming.

The tiny earpiece of his radio was crackling at him, and Jack Grimaldi's familiar voice seemed to emanate from somewhere inside his ringing skull. Bolan eased back on the launcher's trigger, cupping a hand over his other ear to screen out the screams of the wounded and dying from below.

"Time to go, Striker. Cavalry's coming."

Bolan grinned and shook his head. He knew better, yeah.

The cavalry had already arrived.

And in the distance now, he could hear the converging sirens. That would be Bob Wilson, leading in the SWAT teams on a mop-up mission. Bolan backed off, leaving the remains to Wilson and his troops.

The Executioner's mind was already racing away from the smoky killing ground toward the final stop along his hellfire journey through Miami.

The soldier had some final business to transact with Toro yet, before he called it quits and started looking for another hellground.

Toro was waiting for him, right, and Mack Bolan could not afford to be late. The fate of his mission could be hanging in the balance, still undecided, and the soldier never left a job unfinished.

Bolan closed his eyes and waited for Grimaldi to find him through the smoke.

23

Raoul Ornelas knew his time was coming. He was seated in the rear of Toro's ancient Cadillac with one of Toro's commandos close behind him. Toro and his wheelman in the front, the renegade was searching for a way to save himself before his captors got down to their final business of the day.

They had not bound his hands or feet, leaving him free to move, but the *soldado* on his right had a Browning 9mm automatic pistol cradled in his lap, its muzzle pointed casually toward the floor. The gunner was pretending to stare distractedly out of the window now, but Ornelas had no doubt of what would happen if he tried to extricate himself.

They had been driving aimlessly around Miami for better than an hour, finally pulling into Lummus Park, just west of the North-South Expressway. The driver nosed the Caddy into a turnout overhung with trees; directly to their front were a barbecue and several deserted picnic tables.

It was a peaceful scene—and they had brought him there to kill him.

Ornelas was sure of it. There was no other explanation. If they had intended to deliver him to the police, he would be looking out through bars right now, instead of staring through a dirty windshield at abandoned picnic tables.

The knowledge that they meant to execute him compelled Ornelas to consider desperate action. They would shoot him if he tried to escape—and if he did not make the effort, they would kill him all the same.

With all the odds against him now, he saw no reason not to try. That they seemed to be waiting for someone or something might provide him with the hairbreadth opportunity he needed to effect his getaway.

Toro's men had searched him at the house, but they had overlooked the hidden knife that he habitually carried. It was disguised as a belt buckle, and its two-inch double-edged blade fit tightly into a built-in sheath, parallel to his waistline. One simple twist, a gentle pull. . . .

Ornelas shifted restlessly on his seat, bringing both hands together in his lap. The gunner beside him did not stir, but Ornelas caught one of the driver's eyes in the rearview mirror pinning him briefly, then looking away. Ornelas's right hand inched up to find the buckle, finally clamped around it, locking down.

Timing was of the essence; he had the slimmest fraction of a chance if he was swift and coordinated enough—if he still had the skill he once possessed when he fought side by side with Toro in the jungles.

A different jungle now, oh yes, and they were no longer *compadres*. The world had turned, and one of them had been left far behind.

Ornelas took a deep breath and held it, clenching his muscles, praying that the guard beside him could not feel him trembling and become alarmed. The blood was pounding in his ears, deafening him. He felt that he might faint at any moment.

A twist and tug. The stainless blade came free, and he

was moving, pivoting in his seat, sweeping the stubby dirk around and over in a vicious two-handed thrust. The gunner was reacting, feeling rather than seeing the death blow as he began his countermove.

The razor tip disappeared into dusky flesh, its passage lubricated by a spill of crimson as Ornelas found the jugular instinctively, ripping back and forth with furious strength, opening the gunner's veins and airway, watching as the wound expelled a single glistening bubble.

The bubble burst as Ornelas withdrew the blade, already craning forward, slashing at Toro in profile as the warrior turned to face him. The knife glanced off a cheekbone, shearing through an eyeball, knicking the bridge of Toro's nose before ripping free. Toro jerked away, bringing one hand up to clasp the spurting wound.

Ornelas never faltered, twisting in his seat again, driving the dagger deep into the hairy base of the wheelman's skull. The driver screamed, his back arching in agony, both hands coming up and back, trying to remove the blade that had been wedged in deep between his vertebrae.

Ornelas left it there, lunging for the Browning that had fallen down between his closest captor's feet. He reached it, thumbed the hammer back, already pushing himself backward, against the door, one hand clawing at the latch while he thrust out the gun with his other.

He shot the back-seat gunman in the temple, taking no chances that he might still be alive. The young man's skull exploded, sending scarlet streamers out the open window beside him.

Now Ornelas had the door open, sweeping on with the pistol and jamming it against the dying driver's skull.

He squeezed the trigger twice, explosive impact hurling the dead man forward, smashing his ruined face against the steering wheel with a resounding thump. Ornelas was deafened by the gun blasts fired in close confinement, his ears ringing.

Toro was turning to face him again, his pistol already nosing up over the back of his seat as Ornelas tumbled backward through the open door. He fired wildly through the seat cushions into Toro's ravaged face, aiming at his one remaining eye and finding it with point-blank rounds. Already dead or dying, Toro got off a single shot that plowed a bloody furrow under Ornelas's left arm, driving him out of the car.

Ornelas sat there for a moment, stunned, then slowly found his feet. He clutched one arm against his side, to stanch the flow of blood from the in-and-out wound in his side.

Cursing, he leaned back inside the car and pumped three more rounds into Toro's lifeless head, finally backing away, faltering. He was giddy with elation at his close escape, already feeling shock from loss of blood. He was alive, damn right, but he would have to find a doctor soon.

He lurched onto the narrow roadway that wound through the park, deserting the Caddy and its lifeless passengers. There was a sound, a movement, something that he knew he should recognize and take into account, but his disordered mind could not assimilate the data pouring in upon him.

MACK BOLAN CAUGHT THE TURNOFF into Lummus Park and shifted down, putting Evangelina's little drop-top through the gears smoothly, powering into a gentle curve. He was looking forward to the meet with Toro and Ornelas. It would be his last chance to get some answers in Miami.

He'd get the final evidence to tie the Cuban embassy and DGI in with the near-atrocity on Key Biscayne, damn right, and once he had it, he would be equipped to place the full responsibility where it belonged.

There were authorities that he could get in touch with, secretly, of course. Some newsmen who would plant a story without asking too many embarrassing questions of the source. But he would need the proof, and Raoul Ornelas was his ticket to the final grand slam in Miami's tournament of death.

Bolan took the little fiery sportster along the curving path that wound in and out through the park, passing a couple of early-morning campers on the way. A tropic sun was burning off the morning mists now, and he knew it was going to be a beautiful day.

For someone, right.

The drive was narrowed down to two lanes when he spied the Cadillac ahead. From fifty yards, he saw some sort of frantic struggle going on inside there. At forty yards a man tumbled backward, out the rear door on the driver's side, exchanging shots with one or another of the occupants.

The gunner rose, firing back inside the car again, then turned to make a break for freedom.

In a flash the Executioner knew exactly what was happening, and who the stranger was. He knew that he was too damned late to put the pieces back in place again, and blind mind-warping fury took over in a heartbeat.

He tromped on the convertible's gas pedal, driven back into his seat by the sudden surge of power, holding the wheel steady and aiming directly for the armed pedestrian who somehow, incredibly, did not seem to hear or see him.

A last-second correction, and he hit the guy dead center, rolling him up across the hood so that his skull impacted on the windshield, cracking the safety glass and staining it with his blood. Ornelas lay draped across the hood like some horrendous hunting trophy when the sportster came to rest another sixty feet along the path.

Bolan exited from the car and jogged back to the Caddy, bending down to glance in through the open doorway at the slaughterhouse inside. He did not have to check for pulses or move the bodies to know he was looking at a carload of corpses.

The Executioner had seen it all before, right, too damn many times.

Bolan straightened up, turning away from that vehicle of death, staring back along the little sports car's track. The flame-red shark was waiting for him there, Raoul Ornelas draped across its nose and going nowhere.

The Executioner felt hollow, drained. The battle for Miami had been too expensive for his taste—and still, he had not reached the end of it.

The was still a tab remaining to be paid for all the carnage, still a debt remaining to be cleared. He knew, with grim certainty, exactly where to send the check.

With long determined strides, he started back in the direction of the sports car.

EPILOGUE

Jorge Ybarra sipped at his champagne and made a mental note to recommend that buyers for the embassy try out a different brand in the future.

He resisted the urge to make a sour face at the insufferable swill, smiling instead at the uncomprehending wife of a minor-league African ambassador. One never knew exactly what emerging nations might regard as an insulting gesture; better to put on a brave face, and be sociable despite the hour and the endless, soporific conversation.

Ybarra was becoming sick of embassy engagements, almost longing for the simpler days when everything was cut and dried, life being lived on the edge of disaster, fighting for something one believed in. The sitting around, the verbal sparring matches, were something that the cultural attaché would never become accustomed to, he knew.

He had not been disheartened by the failure of his plans for Key Biscayne. The *marielistas* were expendable, of course, and no one in Havana—or in Moscow, for that matter—would be likely to protest his cash expenditures considering the propaganda they could make from open warfare in the streets.

It had not been a total waste, although the knowledge of his failure had been personally unsettling. One did not advance upward through the ranks by watching long-term plans disintegrate.

He wondered just exactly how the Mafia had tumbled to his plan, and why the ranking local *capo* had decided to interfere. It made no sense, but then again, the gangster's presence at the killing scene had guaranteed some headlines for the bungled coup.

Not as many as it would have rated with successful executions, naturally, but still, it was better than nothing.

The waiter, Andres, appeared to rescue him from the midst of an interminable joke the Africans were trying to complete with no success. There was a phone call for him, and the caller would give no name other than Jose, insisting that he must speak with the cultural attaché at once.

Ybarra graciously excused himself, feigning minor irritation as he made his apologies to the African delegation. In truth, he was looking forward to some words with Raoul Ornelas, a chance to be rid of the dreadful champagne once and for all.

He told Andres curtly that he would take the call in his office, already moving for the stairs, brushing through the tuxedoed crowd at a fast walking pace.

He mounted the stairs, rehearsing in his mind exactly what he planned to tell Ornelas. The man deserved a reprimand, but yet, if he escaped arrest on this fiasco, he might still be useful in the future.

Ybarra reached his office door, unlocked it with the special key that he alone possessed. No other cultural attaché in the world was quite so jealous of his secrets as the slim man from Havana.

He closed the door behind him, lost in the gloom for a

moment until he found the light switch, flicked it on. After the darkness of the tomb, it took his eyes an instant to adjust—but he immediately saw that there was something wrong.

His eyes narrowed against the sudden glare, and he discerned something on his desk, a bulky object...not unlike a football. He took a closer step, frowning...and he recognized the severed head of one Raoul Ornelas, wide eyes gaping at him sightlessly, the mouth twisted into one last grimace, hair matted down with drying blood.

Ybarra felt the scream rising in his throat, but vomit choked it off. He was gagging, backing away from the desk on unsteady legs, when a subtle scraping sound behind him alerted him to danger.

He spun around, mouth dropping open at the sight of a tall man, dressed in skintight black, emerging from behind the open office door. The intruder's face was blackened with cosmetics, eyes as cold as death itself— and the automatic pistol in his rising fist was silencer-equipped.

Jorge Ybarra never heard the shot that killed him.

DON PENDLETON'S EXECUTIONER
MACK BOLAN

Sergeant Mercy in Nam . . . The Executioner in the Mafia Wars . . . Colonel John Phoenix in the Terrorist Wars. . . . Now Mack Bolan fights his loneliest war! You've never read writing like this before. Faceless dogsoldiers have killed April Rose. The Executioner's one link with compassion is broken. His path is clear: by fire and maneuver, he will rack up hell in a world shock-tilted by terror. Bolan wages unsanctioned war—everywhere!

GOLD
EAGLE

Available wherever paperbacks are sold.

Mack Bolan's

ABLE TEAM

by Dick Stivers

Action writhes in the reader's own street as Able Team's Carl "Mr. Ironman" Lyons, Pol Blancanales and Gadgets Schwarz make triple trouble in blazing war. To these superspecialists, justice is as sharp as a knife. Join the guys who began it all—Dick Stivers's Able Team!

"This guy has a fertile mind and a great eye for detail. Dick Stivers is brilliant!"

—*Don Pendleton*

Able Team titles are available wherever paperbacks are sold.

GOLD EAGLE

Mack Bolan's

PHOENIX FORCE

by Gar Wilson

Schooled in guerilla warfare, equipped with all the latest lethal hardware, Phoenix Force battles the powers of darkness in an endless crusade for freedom, justice and the rights of the individual. Follow the adventures of one of the legends of the genre. Phoenix Force is the free world's foreign legion!

"Gar Wilson is excellent! Raw action attacks the reader on every page."

—*Don Pendleton*

#1 Argentine Deadline
#2 Guerilla Games
#3 Atlantic Scramble
#4 Tigers of Justice
#5 The Fury Bombs
#6 White Hell
#7 Dragon's Kill

#8 Aswan Hellbox
#9 Ultimate Terror
#10 Korean Killground
#11 Return to Armageddon
#12 The Black Alchemists
#13 Harvest Hell
#14 Phoenix in Flames

Phoenix Force titles are available wherever paperbacks are sold.

GOLD EAGLE